a novella

KEV HARRISON
THE BALANCE

THE BALANCE

Kev Harrison

Dear Amanda,
hope you dig it.
Best,

LVP
PUBLICATIONS

Lycan Valley Press Publications
1625 E 72nd St STE 700 PMB 132
Tacoma, Washington 98404 United States of America

Printed in the United States of America

First Edition, April 2020

ISBN-13: 978-1-64562-985-6

To the young people in my various classrooms in Poland.
You taught me as much as I taught you.
I hope for a bright, balanced future for you all.
Thank you.

CHAPTER 1

NATALIA carried her brother's limp body into the house. "Mum, mum, quick! Kuba's hurt!"

Her mother's cheeks were flushed as she came dashing in from the back garden, her face wrought with panic. She looked at her son's body, motionless but for the shallow movement of his chest as he inhaled and exhaled. She shot daggers at her daughter and spat, "What the hell happened? What's the matter with him?"

Her eyes followed Natalia's to the boy's ankle, twisted at an awkward angle, the crimson stain of blood already colouring his trainers. Natalia sniffed, still adjusting to being inside from the frozen cold, and looked at her mother, her eyes pleading. "We went to the woods. I was watching him the whole time, then I saw some flowers." She sniffed and scrunched her eyes shut for a moment, to prevent herself from crying. Then she carried on. "I called to him to follow me, but he didn't. I didn't know he was in the tree until…"

"Stupid girl!" Her mother's eyes were fixed on Natalia's, unblinking. "And how did he come to be out cold, can you tell me that?" She put her hand to her son's head, checking for fever.

Natalia's skin went pale. "I think it's shock. The bone…" And then she broke, tears streaming down her face.

Their mother untied the shoelace quickly but carefully and slipped the shoe from his foot. The swelling was great, but more disturbing was the visible fragment of bone, strands of bloodied muscle tissue clinging to it. She crossed herself, eyes closed, then turned to Natalia. "Go to the village. Get the doctor."

Natalia wiped her nose with the back of her hand and nodded. She started to back out of the box-like bedroom. "Mum, I'm so sorry."

"Just go!" Now was not the time for conversation.

Natalia stepped back out into the frozen yard at the front of the house, tying her scarf tightly around her neck and pulling her hat down to cover her ears. Her heavy boots crunched through the densely packed snow, every step cutting into the silence that hung ominously over everything. The doctor's cottage was less than a kilometre away. But for the handful of children that still lived out here in the village, no one was foolish enough to be outside in such frigid weather.

She walked past the copse that led into the dense forest where her younger brother had fallen and wrung her hands, the guilt at having taken her eyes from him gnawing at her, like a rat at the bones of festering carrion. The sun was setting now, her shadow long on the glittering snow ahead. Dark shapes moved in the woodland, the sound of snapping twigs emanating periodically from beyond the visible first line of trees. No one in the village dared enter by night. It was a wild place where old things, not of this world, held dominion.

She picked up her pace, marching now, onward towards the other houses, whose early evening firelight she could see, wisps of wood smoke perfuming the crisp winter air. The silhouette of the carpenter's wife looked out, as ever, from their window as she passed. Natalia wondered what the interfering old gossip would make of what had happened today. How she might frame the story in the rabble outside the church on Sunday.

Natalia came to the village square, looking up at the sandstone-clad tower of the church looming over her, the sole building more than two storeys high. She crossed herself as she looked up at the carved angel above the main door, saying a few words of silent prayer for her brother. Then turned right and hurried along the roughly-hewn path which led up to the doctor's house. She rapped on the wooden door with her knuckles, the impact stinging her frozen fingers.

She waited for a long moment, then heard movement from inside the house, the sound of wooden furniture creaking on floorboards. The door was unlocked, the bolt pulled back and Doctor Malinowski opened the door. Golden firelight grew from a sliver to a wide portal, stark against the darkening scenery, and illuminated the old doctor's face as it creased into a smile.

"Natalia," he said in his slow, considered manner. "It's not the best weather for a walk. What can I do for you? Would you like to come in?" He stepped back a little, beckoning her towards the hearth with his left hand, while his right clutched the bolt on the door.

Natalia tried to force a smile, but surrendered. "Doctor Malinowski, it's Kuba. He fell and hurt his leg. I think it's broken."

The gentle smile on the old man's face receded. "Are you quite sure it's broken, my dear? It might just be a sprain or a twist."

Natalia shook her head, biting her lip. "You can see the bone, Doctor."

Malinowski reached around to the hook behind the front door, returning to Natalia's sight with his leather bag and long coat. He sat down and put on his snow boots, fixing the cast iron grate in front of the fire before stepping out in to the growing night. "You can tell me what happened on the way, all right?"

Natalia nodded and began to explain. The ink of

night had bled across the sky by the time they arrived back at the house. Only the twinkling starlight, reflected off the dazzling snow, showed them the way. Natalia's mother was waiting by the window, and Natalia felt her eyes boring into her as they followed the path up to the door.

The door swung open as they approached and Natalia's mother stepped out, offering her hand to the doctor.

He shook it and held it with a firm grip. "It's going to be all right, Beata. Try to stay calm."

"It's hard to stay calm, Doctor. He's my baby boy. He's been in and out of consciousness the whole time. The pain must be dreadful." She pulled her hand back and clasped it to the other.

"I understand, really, I do. Now, get some vodka for the pain. If you have any clean cloth, we'll likely have to fashion a bandage for him. Supplies are… sparse, as well you know. Natalia, you come with me, I could use an extra pair of hands." He looked at the young girl, beaming a smile at her.

Natalia nodded and led him into the boy's bedroom, while her mother scuttled off towards the kitchen.

The doctor peeled back the sheets and blankets that covered the boy and stared at his ruined ankle, his trouser leg rolled up away from the wound. "Goodness, the landing must have been very heavy." The doctor seemed to be speaking aloud to himself, but Natalia sounded her agreement anyway. "Can you get me some hot water, my dear?" he said.

Natalia sprang to action, running to the kitchen and almost sending her mother crashing to the ground, vodka bottle and all. "I'm sorry, Mum. I need hot water. For the doctor."

Her mother shoved the bottle and the cloth into Natalia's arms. "Take these, I'll get the water."

Natalia clutched the items close to her chest and headed back into the room, where Malinowski was on his knees, trying to push the bone back up, under the torn muscle from where it had come. He looked up at Natalia.

"Natalia, can you put two fingers, like this?" He showed her with his free left hand, his first two fingers held together. "I want you to put them just behind the knee joint, and feel if there's any movement in or around the socket when I push the bone up. It might be a bit strange. Can you do that for me?"

Natalia nodded, placing the vodka bottle and the makeshift bandage material on top of the old hardwood chest of drawers beside the bed. She made the shape with her fingers, as she'd been shown, and pressed. The doctor shoved the bone back into the wound and she felt it grinding as it pressed against the knee socket. She called out, "Doctor," but before she could say any more, Kuba was awake, his mouth a gaping vision of pain as a low groan escaped him.

Natalia's mother came dashing into the room.

"What's happening?" Her face contorted with fear and confusion.

The doctor looked around to her. "It's to be expected, we're forcing the bone back into place. I think we're going to have to give him vodka for the pain. Beata, can you give him some? Just a drop."

Natalia's mother's eyes looked haunted, but she nodded and reached for the bottle, unscrewing the cap. "How much should I give him? He's ten years old, for goodness' sake."

"Quite right," Malinowksi said. "About half a cup should inebriate him sufficiently to take the edge off the pain. Then be sure to bring that water, all right?"

Beata was already moving the cup to her prone child, tipping it to his lips and leaning his head forward with her free hand. He coughed as the burning liquor went down and she paused before giving him the rest of the dose. She supported his head, lowering it back onto his pillow, and wiped the liquid from around his lips. "I'll get the water," she said and scurried out of the room.

The doctor looked up to Natalia once more. "Ready to try again?"

Natalia nodded, pressing her fingers against the base of the knee. The doctor gripped the calf from underneath this time and then shoved the bone back in. Natalia's stomach became a squalling sea of sickness as she felt the end of the bone grind itself into place in his knee socket. She managed to force out the words, "I think it's all right now, Doctor."

The doctor smiled, then called out, "We're going to need the water now, Beata."

She was already at the bedroom door, hands clasped around a basin of hot water, steam billowing from the top. She placed it down on top of the chest of drawers, beside the vodka and bandage material Natalia had brought earlier.

The doctor stood and dipped a cloth he had taken from his medical bag into the steaming fluid and cleaned the wound. Mud, dried blood and melted snow had gathered around the torn skin. He rinsed it and cleaned it again, dropping the cloth into the steaming water. "Now a little vodka to sterilise the wound," he said under his breath. He took the lid from the bottle and dribbled a little of the alcohol over the boy's injury, before gesturing for Natalia to bring the bandage.

She held up the leg as the doctor wrapped the bandage around over and over again, until the wound was compressed tight. Their mother just crouched at the head of the bed, wiping sweat from her young son's brow. After a few minutes, their work was done.

"I've tea in the pot, Doctor, if you'd like some," Natalia's mother said, calmer now.

Malinowski nodded, sealing up his bag and resting it against the wall near the door to Kuba's room. Natalia joined them at the table, all sitting in front of steaming, aromatic cups.

"Is he going to be all right?" Beata's hands still shook as she lifted her teacup to take a sip.

"Well, there's no reason the bone won't heal. It was a clean break. Now that the splinter of bone has been put back in the right place, it should fuse well enough. Though the boy won't walk on it for at least a couple weeks."

"Oh thank the Lord-"

"What worries me, though, is the wound," he said. "With a cut so deep, I'd like to use antibiotics. But I don't have any in my stores—indeed there aren't nearly enough in all of Poland—and there's no way I can get a delivery through here until the snow has melted. The risk of infection is… troubling."

Natalia shook her head gravely, as she felt her mother's eyes bore into her. The three of them finished their tea in silence and then her mother showed the doctor out.

CHAPTER 2

Five days passed relatively uneventfully, Kuba getting out of bed only when he needed to use the toilet. Natalia's sense of remorse at what had happened in the forest grew stronger every time she saw him dragging his injured leg to the bathroom and back. On the second afternoon she brought him a sturdy length of wood the carpenter had no use for, which he could use as a crutch. Kuba said he was grateful and that Natalia shouldn't blame herself for his falling out of the tree. Their mother had other ideas, though.

Natalia was clearing away the crockery from her brother's dinner in the evening—he was eating propped up in bed, so that his leg remained elevated —when her mother rushed in. "Don't think for one moment that you're free now, young lady. Once you've washed those things up, you'll be back here to help me change the dressing."

Natalia nodded as she shuffled out of the room, being careful not to drop anything and get herself in yet more trouble. She poured water from the boiling pan on the stove into a basin and carried it carefully into her brother's room. She placed it on the chest of drawers and hurried back to the kitchen to get clean fabric for the new bandage. She almost dropped the material onto the tiled floor when she heard her mother screaming. She rushed back into the room.

The swelling around the ankle had reduced a huge amount, but the torn skin was a deep, bluish purple. The scar tissue had a green tinge where it was growing back together. As Malinowski had predicted, the wound seemed to be infected.

"Do you feel unwell? Feverish?" Their mother placed the back of her hand against Kuba's forehead.

The boy shook his head vigorously. "I actually feel much better. The pain is less than yesterday." He looked toward Natalia and smiled.

"Mum, should I fetch the doctor again?" Natalia was already walking down the short hallway to fetch her coat. She came back to the bedroom door, stuffing her right arm into the thick, padded sleeve. Her mother was standing, waiting for her. She grabbed her wrist firmly and led her into the kitchen. She motioned to the clock on the mantel.

"The doctor? At almost ten at night, in this weather?" It came across as a taunt more than a question. "I sometimes wish the Lord had seen fit to give you brains, girl."

Natalia looked into her mother's eyes. "I just want to help my brother, that's all." Her heart thumped in her chest, the low-pitched drumming of blood swimming up to her ears in a dull, monotonous thud. "Is there anything we can do?"

Her mother stalked across the kitchen to one of the old, dilapidated cupboards and pulled out the vodka bottle. "We'll put some of this onto the wound again. My grandfather never had any antibiotics, not even when Grandma Dorota had to cut shrapnel from his hip. Just a hot knife and strong spirits. Come on."

Natalia followed and watched, her brother's face twisting as the alcohol burned the raw flesh of the wound. She crouched down and helped her mother as she'd helped the doctor a few days before. They applied the cotton, maintaining constant pressure on the wound. Natalia went back to the room she shared with her mother and climbed into bed, ignoring the older woman's prayers.

The sun was just peeking over the horizon when Natalia stepped out into the blinding whiteness. Here in the east, in mid-winter, the cold was a tangible enemy, biting at you from the moment you stepped away from the fire. Even with a vest, a thick woollen jumper and her heavy, quilted coat, she felt permeated by the thick frost as she trudged into the village. Fresh snow had dusted the plains overnight, so the paths she trod were from memory more than any visible markings on the frozen earth.

Doctor Malinowski agreed to come immediately, once he heard about the state of Kuba's wound. Since Mrs. Malinowska's death, the doctor barely kept to any sort of timetable, instead choosing to live out his remaining years in service to the village where he'd always lived, doing the best he could with what limited resources he had. On the walk back to the house, he questioned Natalia, asking for a more detailed description of the state of the cut, about whether Kuba had experienced chills or hot flushes. She told him what she could, but the severity of his tone frightened her.

Kuba is going to recover, isn't he?

Again, her mother was waiting to greet them, distress etched on her face even more gravely than it had been on the day of the accident. The doctor seemed not to be perturbed by her and stepped through to the boy's room, immediately beginning to check his vital signs. He worked briskly for twenty minutes, taking a note of blood pressure, temperature, heart rate and, of course, the state of the wound itself.

"You did the right thing to use the vodka again," he said, resting his stethoscope around his shoulders. "I checked in my stores and, as I feared, there are no antibiotics. I went yesterday to the post office and sent a telegram to the hospital in Lublin, but I don't suppose they'll be much better off—you know how it is with the Soviet government. And even if they were, I'm not sure how the medicine might get here with snows every night." He nodded toward the pure white drift mounting up behind Kuba's window.

Natalia and her mother both followed him into the kitchen where he went to wash his hands with hot water, which he ladled into a basin from the cauldron-like pan on the stove.

"What can we do now, doctor?" Natalia's mother's usually confident voice warbled with fear. She arched her neck around the kitchen door towards Kuba's bedroom, then continued in a hushed tone. "What if it doesn't get better?"

The doctor dried his hands on a towel hanging over the back of a chair and turned to face them both. "If the infection spreads... Well, in the worst case we would have to amputate." Natalia gasped, fixing her hands over her lips. The doctor's look softened into a smile. "It's not going to go that far, I'm quite sure. But I want to prepare you for the worst. And amputation is a hell of a lot better than septicaemia."

Natalia looked over at her mother, whose skin was pale, eyes heavy with the lack of sleep. Her mother reached out to the doctor, taking his right hand in both of hers. "Thank you for everything you've done, Doctor. You'll tell us if you do receive any medication, won't you?"

The doctor nodded his head. "But in the meantime, homemade vodka is the next best thing. Fetch me if things develop for the worse." Natalia watched him with no small amount of concern as he strode to the front door, put on his coat and hat and let himself out, the heavy door slamming shut behind him.

She'd allowed her brother to sleep, as her mother instructed, until lunchtime. Now, with her mother in the village at her part-time job at the small linen factory, Natalia was preparing soup for herself and Kuba. She lifted the wooden spoon to her lips, tasting the purplish liquid. She smacked her lips, trying to decide what was missing. She laid the spoon across the top of the wide pan and walked across the kitchen, returning with a sprig of marjoram from the bundle she'd brought back from the forest. She tore the leaves and dropped them into the barszcz, the delicate fragrance filling the air as she stirred the bubbling liquid.

She tried it again and, now satisfied with the flavour, she began to ladle the soup into wooden bowls. She planted Kuba's bowl onto a metallic tray and tore off a hunk from the fresh loaf in the breadbin, which she placed next to the bowl. She carried the tray into Kuba's room. "Hey, dozy, time for some food," she said as she placed the tray down on the bedside table.

Kuba opened his eyes, releasing a yawn and stretching. He dragged himself up the bed, careful not to put undue strain on the injured ankle, and then angled his pillow so he could sit up straight. He pulled the blankets high up his torso. "What are we having?" He looked up to the steam rising from his bowl and the crusty bread at the side.

"Beetroot soup," Natalia said as she lowered the tray onto his lap, careful not to spill any. The boy gripped his spoon and dipped it in, blew on it and then took a sip. "Do you like it?" Natalia asked him, ever keen to make amends for his injury. He nodded his head and ripped a piece of the bread off, dipping it and stuffing it into his mouth, the liquid running down his chin.

Natalia rubbed his hair with her hand and was walking towards the door when her brother called out to her. "Natka!" She spun around.

"What is it, Kuba?" She hurried back to his bedside.

He looked up at her. "Will you eat in here with me today? It's boring being alone all the time." He stuffed another chunk of soup-soaked bread into his mouth.

Natalia beamed at him and held up her index finger. "One minute," she said, and dashed to the kitchen. She came back with her lunch and moved the wooden chair to one side of his desk, sitting down and beginning to eat. "How are you feeling now?"

Kuba shrugged his shoulders. "It still hurts a little bit, but I forget the pain when I'm eating." He flashed her a broad grin, the dark soup staining his lips. "But, Natka, I'm so cold today. Sweating, but frozen. Even with the heat from the fire and all these blankets." He tugged at his heavy bedclothes with his left hand.

Natalia felt her stomach begin to churn, but forced another mouthful of soup down, not wanting to scare the boy. "Have you mentioned this to Mum yet?"

Kuba picked up the bowl with both hands and drank down the remnants of his lunch. He wiped his mouth with the back of his hand and then shook his head. "I can't tell Mum; she's already convinced I'm going to die. You know Tomasz, the station master's son?" When Natalia nodded, he went on. "Well, he dislocated his ankle and he was still allowed to come out to the lake with us last summer. Mum worries too much."

Natalia thought about another spoonful of soup but couldn't manage it. She put the spoon down in the bowl and sighed. "Look, little brother, Mum *is* a nightmare. I know better than you, trust me. But since Dad left, she's had a miserable time. And she worries about you because you're the man of the house now, you know?"

Kuba moved the tray with the empty bowl and breadcrumbs over to his bedside table. "I know all that. But I'm ten. I want to be out in the snow. And I'll be fine." He slapped his leg.

Natalia nodded, standing to gather the dirty things. She took them into the kitchen and washed them up. Silent tears rolled down her nose and dripped into the water, tiny ripples emanating outwards.

CHAPTER 3

THE SUN was sinking below the horizon behind the forest when their mother arrived home. She came into the kitchen humming a tune to herself, seemingly in much better sorts than she had been over the past few days.

Natalia moved the soup pan over the heat again and, when it started to bubble, served a portion to her mother, who sat at the table. "How was work?" she asked as she sat opposite.

Beata began to eat the soup, clearly hungry. She looked up after a moment. "This is really tasty, Natalia, thank you. Work was normal. It's not much fun embroidering for four hours a day, but it brings us a little money." She dunked her bread and took a bite. "How's your brother?" she asked after she'd swallowed it down.

Natalia lowered her eyes. "He's in really good spirits. Ate all his lunch, and I even ate with him, so we could chat a bit."

"That's good, he's feeling better," her mother

said, lifting the bowl with two hands and drinking the soup down.

"But he's got chills. Sweats, too. I think we'll need to get Malinowski to look at him again." Natalia stood, collecting her mother's dirty dishes and walking over to the sink to clean them.

"Jesus and Mary," her mother said, her chair making a grinding sound against the floor as she stood. "I'll go now. Go and check on him when you're done here, please."

By the time Natalia finished washing out the inside of her mother's bowl and turned around, Beata was already wrapping her scarf around her neck. She waved and opened the door, stepping out into the growing darkness.

Natalia dried her hands and crept around to Kuba's room. He was fast asleep. She stepped across the floorboards to stand above him, reaching down with her hand. His skin was cold and clammy. She brought the other hand up to cover her mouth. The infection. She walked out of the room and back to the room she shared with her mother. She knelt down in front of the cross, mounted high up on the wall, closed her eyes and began to pray under her breath. For her forgiveness and for her brother's recovery. Neither of which she was sure would be forthcoming.

She was stretched out on her bed, reading, when she heard the front door burst open. The heavy, direct footsteps of her mother were followed by the quieter, but no less urgent pacing of the doctor.

Natalia dashed into the room to observe as he once again drew a series of instruments from his bag, and performed checks, confirming that the boy was indeed feverish.

"We can't be sure it's the leg though. It's the middle of winter; infections with symptoms like these could be anything. It's probably just a heavy cold. Let's take off the dressing and see." His eyes moved from Natalia to her mother and back as he tried to reassure them both.

It immediately became clear that this was no cold. The laceration gave off a rank smell the moment the bandage was removed and had a greenish tinge to it.

The doctor's face fell. "I'm afraid this infection appears to be serious. What's worse, see the line here?" He gestured to a dark line under the skin, multiple bluish vein-like tendrils growing away from it under the skin. "This indicates the infection is spreading. I'll go to the post office immediately and petition once again for antibiotics, but, if they are not forthcoming…"

"You'll have to take my leg?" Kuba's skin was sallow, prune-coloured bags drooping beneath his eyes. His voice trembled with fear. It was not something a ten-year-old should ever have to face.

The doctor reached out to hold Kuba's hand, no doubt noticing the chill temperature of the boy's flesh. He nodded. "My fear, young man, is if we don't, the infection could spread to your blood. If that happens, you could lose far more than your leg."

The time for pulling punches had long since

passed, it seemed. Natalia balled her hands into fists, feeling physically distant from what was happening, removed somehow. She looked at the doctor to one side and her mother to the other, their voices unintelligible echoes in her head, then to her baby brother, not long ten years old and about to become a cripple. Because of her. Because she had not paid attention. It couldn't be like this. It couldn't.

Two days passed, the doctor yet to confirm whether the antibiotics would be supplied or not. Natalia had tried to talk to her mother several times about the incident, about the amputation, but her mother had dismissed her each time.

"Don't waste your breath talking to me. Only God can forgive you."

The same reply over and over again. Until the second night. The two of them sat in the kitchen after dinner. Kuba's fever had subsided somewhat, the chills receding and allowing him to rest in relative comfort. The wound continued to ooze odorous pus, which existed as a silent taunt of what was to happen to him.

Beata spoke first. "I'm growing impatient, waiting for news from the doctor," she said, worry etched onto her face. "If we don't hear by tomorrow evening, I'm going to send you to his house, all right?"

Natalia shrugged. "Fine with me. Anything I can do to help Kuba." She returned to her book, her eyes following her finger as she traced her way down the page in the low, flickering candlelight. Then she stopped reading, closing the book. "Mum, I wanted to ask you something. What if there was another way to help him? Someone that could do more to help than the doctor, with his limited supplies?"

Her mother sipped her lukewarm tea and then spoke under her breath. "Do tell me what you've thought of that none of us have over the last week."

Natalia thought better of biting back and stood up, pouring herself a cup of tea from the pot which sat on the stove. "I could take him to Baba Yaga," she said, the words almost a whisper.

Her mother sprang to her feet, her tea cup falling over and the liquid creeping toward Natalia's book. They both watched, motionless, as it seeped into the grains of the table and edged ever closer, then began to run the length of the spine as it made contact. Natalia stepped forward to rescue the book, seemingly bringing her mother back to Earth.

"Baba Yaga? Not enough that you would cost your brother one of his limbs through your negligence, but you'd damn him with black magic and mumbo jumbo, too?" She paced the length of the kitchen, to the back door of the cottage and back. "Heaven knows what she would do to him. Never heard of human sacrifice, girl? Has church taught you nothing?"

Natalia bit her lip, not wanting to let her anger get the better of her. She breathed in deeply, then fixed her eyes on her mother's. "Grandma used to go to her for all kinds of things. Medicine, tea infusions. I remember she took me to her house once."

Her mother threw her hands up in the air. "Such

revelations, now of all times. My daughter suckled at the witch's teat. Was it before or after Lucifer? Tell me, girl!" She was shouting, her cheeks flushed, saliva sputtering from her lips as she spat the words.

Natalia laughed to herself and untied her long hair, rubbing her fingertips on her scalp. "You're being utterly ridiculous, Mum. She's not in league with Satan. She's just someone who remembers the old ways. Before all this technology." She gestured towards the long-broken transistor radio on the kitchen counter. "All I'm saying is she might have something. Something which could be a substitute for the antibiotics that Doctor Malinowski can't get hold of." She sat back down in her chair, knitting her fingers together. "Something that might help Kuba." Natalia brushed a tear away from her cheek and looked at her silent mother imploringly.

The older woman looked deep into her eyes, her sorrow at everything her son was yet to suffer written in her expression. She closed her eyes and shook her head, swallowing. "I will not exchange Jakub's immortal soul for his leg. We'll talk no more of this. You shall sleep on the couch here tonight. I'll not have you near me with this talk of witchcraft. I hope a night's sleep will see you right."

She picked up the knocked-over tea cup and placed it in the sink, then blew out all but one of the burning candles and stormed from the kitchen into their room, closing the door firmly behind her.

Natalia moved the small step ladder and reached up to the high linen cupboard, pulling down a blanket. She lay on the old couch and wrapped herself in it before blowing out the last candle.

CHAPTER 4

NATALIA woke early from an uncomfortable night of fitful sleep. She soaked oats in milk and water for everyone to eat for breakfast. She served herself first, heating the mixture in a dark, cast iron pan and adding a spoonful of wild blackberry jam before eating. When her mother entered the kitchen, she left. They passed the morning in much the same way until her mother left for work.

She waited until the shape of her mother had disappeared out of sight and then hurried into Kuba's room, a collection of his winter clothes tucked under her arm. She dropped them on to the bed, waking her brother up with a jolt. "Fancy going for a walk?"

He sat up and rubbed his eyes. "Where are we going, Natka?" he asked through a long yawn.

"We're going back into the woods," Natalia said, grinning at him. She clapped her hands, urging him to hurry and get dressed.

Kuba looked up at her, an uncertain expression

on his face. "Mum says I shouldn't go outside. And I shouldn't put too much weight on this leg while it's healing." He motioned down to his heavily bandaged ankle with his hands.

Natalia's grin grew still further across her face. "Not going to be a problem," she said. "I'll be right back." She dashed out of the room, then returned wheeling the barrow their mother used to collect potatoes and beets in front of her. Kuba eyed her and the wheelbarrow suspiciously. "Don't worry," Natalia said. "You're still little. You'll fit. Hurry up now."

Pushing the single-wheeled barrow through deep snow with a load of one ten-year-old boy and a few kilos of blankets to keep him warm was far harder work than Natalia had ever anticipated. She pushed and shoved, the muscles in her forearms burning with the effort. After a few minutes, she turned to look back. They couldn't have been more than a few hundred metres from the cottage.

"Why are we going to the forest anyway?" Kuba twisted his face up from under his covering of woollen material.

"We're going to see someone. About your leg." She began to shove him forward again, the sound of the wheel rotating and getting stuck in the densely packed snow cutting through the silent air. Kuba pulled the blanket up to cover his face and looked ahead once more, his gloved fingers gripping the edges of the barrow as Natalia pushed it over the uneven ground.

The sun was high in the almost cloudless blue sky. Tiny particles of ice refracted the light in brilliant rainbow colours as they floated from the branches of the trees on the breeze. They were entering the copse now, the spindly fingers of trees shorn of their summer plumage jutting in all directions and casting shadows at unnerving angles. From the copse they stepped into the forest proper, the evergreens that dominated the area still proudly wearing their coats of needles and flat, tendril-like leaves. The air was fresh with the aromatic scent of torn bark and sap, while the virgin snow of the village terrain was replaced by a confluence of tracks, the meandering footsteps of deer, hares and foxes.

Even as the light was blocked out by the conical towers of pine and fir, the air temperature was noticeably warmer, abundant life and shelter from the wind tempering winter's bite. They were stepping further into the forest than either of them had ever trod alone. From somewhere deep in her distant memories, Natalia could remember treading the same path with her grandmother, as a young girl.

"What will we do if we can't find our way back?" Kuba called out the question, looking up over the tip of his blankets. "We'll be stuck here in the forest. We could be eaten."

Natalia laughed. "I remember the way. I've been here once before. A long time ago." She pointed at something ahead. "You can see the house from here, look."

About seventy-five metres away was a squat stone

cottage, the dark stone long covered with lichens and thick moss. Wispy smoke rose from the chimney and light flickered behind the dulled glass of the windows. Natalia picked up her pace, excitement at finally making it to the house flooding her with adrenaline. Then she stopped.

Beside the door of the house, a large feline shape crouched, back legs folded underneath itself. The lynx licked one of its forepaws, wiping blood from the tufts of fur around its face. Natalia lowered the barrow to the ground and bent down to her brother. "Don't make a sound," she whispered.

The cat's eyes widened, the pupils dilating in an instant so that there was little more than a sliver of amber around pointed almonds of obsidian. Natalia could see the creature's flat nose sniffing at the air.

If it senses Kuba is injured, it might...

The russet wooden door creaked open before she could entertain the thought. An old woman stepped out onto the doorstep, her face covered by a wild tangle of hair. A frail looking hand reaching out from under a frayed fleece shirt and caressed the lynx under the chin. The animal rolled its neck to one side like a house cat, its eyes closed. Then it stood and slinked silently off into the underbrush.

"You don't need to be afraid. He's a friend. And he's already eaten today." The old woman's voice was quiet, yet seemed to travel in perfect clarity across the space between them. Still, Natalia couldn't see her eyes behind the mop of ragged hair. "If you want me to help the boy, you'd best come inside." She turned and walked back into the house, leaving the door wide open.

"Natka, I don't-"

"Quiet! This is your best chance. Or do you want to be a cripple?" Natalia lifted the handles of the barrow and began to push him towards the house. "I'd never put you in danger. I promise, little brother." She looked down at the bloody remains of the hare left on the doorstep by the lynx and hoped she was right as she pushed the barrow inside.

"On the bench over there, quickly, girl," the woman said, her hair scrunched back now, revealing a long face with high cheekbones and an old, heavy scar on the left side of her jaw. "What happened to his leg?"

Natalia lowered Kuba as gently as possible on to the long bench and then spun around, her eyes lingering on tools, plants and bones, strewn on shelves or mounted on walls. "He fell from a tree. I was supposed to be watching him. The bone was... was sticking right out. The doctor fixed it, and the swelling is going down, but now it's infected. He says he'll have to cut off the leg."

The woman brought her face closely over Kuba's and smiled, baring her browned, rotted teeth. "Don't much fancy a stick where your leg used to be, eh lad?" Kuba shook his head violently, his eyes wide with horror. "Don't blame you." She rolled up his trouser leg and unravelled the scarf Natalia had wrapped around his ankle to keep it warm, then untied the bandage. The rank odour wafted up from the wound once again and clear, greenish pus coated the entire area of the cut.

The old woman whistled when she saw it, her fingers tracing the lines of the infection, where they spread up from the laceration and into the tissues above. "Girl! What has your doctor been using on this? It looks rancid."

Natalia tore her eyes from a crow skull above the front door and turned to face the woman. "He wanted antibiotics. But he didn't have any. We've been using vodka to keep it sterile. But it's not working and now…" She started sniffing and then felt the woman's bony hand gripping her shoulder.

"Tears will not help, child. But I have a few things that might. Put your scarf back on and go outside. Cut me some peppermint from the back of the house." She handed her a short, curved blade which she seemed to produce from nowhere and then hurried across the room to a set of shelves, stacked high with jars of glass and ceramics. She began picking them up and setting them back down, as Natalia stepped out into the cold.

She walked around to the back of the house, keeping her eyes sharp for the return of the lynx from earlier. Instead she saw two fat wood pigeons courting on a branch. She found a collection of earthenware pots behind the house, elevated from the frozen ground with thin rope. She rubbed her fingers on the leaves of the plants, smelling her chilled fingertips and recognising first oregano and then the peppermint the old lady had asked for. She cut off a sprig and dashed back into the house.

"Baba Yaga, is this enough?" Natalia called out as she hurried back into the kitchen, which she now noticed better resembled a laboratory. The old woman was pounding at what looked like wood bark with a pestle and mortar. She nodded and tipped the stone bowl forward, urging Natalia to drop it in. She did as she was asked and peered at the bark, now halfway broken down into powder. "What is that stuff?"

The woman looked up, her eyes wildly blue, and said. "Cinnamon. Smell!" She offered the pestle to Natalia who breathed in the exotic fragrance for the first time.

"Hmmmm… weird," Natalia said.

Baba Yaga laughed at her response, but then nodded her agreement. "We need one more ingredient. Can you bring me the honey?" She flicked her head in the direction of some shelves at the other side of the candlelit room, beyond where Kuba was lying, his eyes darting from one specimen to another.

Natalia scurried over and reached up to the shelf. She pulled down a wide, low jar and watched as the viscose liquid glooped one way and then the other as she carried it back to the old lady. Baba Yaga unscrewed the lid and poured a dollop of the golden substance into the mixture. She put the jar down and began pounding again.

"We're ready," the woman said, a few moments later. She carried the pestle and mortar over to where Kuba was laying on the bench. She brought her bony fingers down to Kuba's wound and prodded at the greenish scar tissue that was trying to grow over at either side. "We need to get this into the cut itself. Can you help me?"

Natalia stepped forward, letting the old woman's frail hands guide hers to either side of the boy's wound. She pushed a little, demonstrating to

Natalia how to prise the scar tissue apart. The vile smell of the infection wafted up, almost making her retch. She looked up at Kuba, his face contorted with concern. "I think this might hurt a bit, brother."

Baba Yaga nodded. "Your sister's right," she said, matter-of-factly. "But when did you ever hear of medicine that tastes like strawberries? Or feels like a fluffy down pillow, eh?" She smiled at him, the deep lines on her face like ancient channels on a dry riverbed. She looked over at Natalia and gave her a nod.

Natalia squeezed the wound open a fraction more and the woman daubed a couple of fingers of the tacky mixture into the cut. She pushed it in, then took another scrape of it from the mortar and sealed up the injury, fixing the bandage he'd come in with back in place.

Natalia looked up at her brother after they had finished, his jaw clamped shut, his eyes slits. "It's over, Kuba. How does it feel?"

He looked down at the bandage, bound around his ankle once more. He shrugged. "I think I'm all right. It felt weird… agonising, then just sticky. But if it'll work…" He shrugged again, using his arms to slide back up the bench and sit upright. "Do we need to go now?"

Natalia had forgotten all about their mother.

Is it possible she's home from work already?

"Do you know what time it is?" she asked.

Baba Yaga walked to the other end of the kitchen, picking up an old pocket watch. "Not yet three in the afternoon," she said. "Are you in trouble?"

Natalia breathed out, relieved. "Mum isn't usually back until after six when she's working. I think we'll be all right." She let herself slide down onto one of the wooden chairs beside the kitchen table.

"If you've three hours, then I'll get some hot tea into you, before I let you back out into the freezing weather." She filled a pot with water, dropping a variety of dried leaves, chips of the cinnamon bark and what looked to Natalia like peppercorns into it. She set it on the stove and lit it, coming away to sit at a chair opposite Natalia. "I've a question for you, young lady." She looked into Natalia's eyes, her hands flat down on the table.

Natalia cocked her head, wondering what an old witch could possibly want to know from a sixteen-year-old girl. "Go on then."

"I want to know why a young girl from a god-fearing village dragged her sick brother into the forest to meet with an old witch."

Natalia swallowed, wondering if this was a challenge. The moment when everything her mother had said about the *witch* in the forest would prove true. She looked down at the table for a moment, her eyes tracing the grain in each plank of wood. "I don't believe you're a servant of Lucifer. I don't even believe in evil things like Satan and demons and what have you."

Baba Yaga reached across the table with a speed that belied her decrepit features, the tip of her index finger pressed under Natalia's chin. She lifted he girl's head until their eyes met. "You *should* believe in demons. And worse besides. It's only the fool who thinks they are safe from the shadows in dark corners."

Natalia shivered.

"But the other part," she went on, "is true. I am not allied to your Satan, nor any of the other dark forces. My role here is one of balance." She retracted her hand from under Natalia's face slowly, more in keeping with her regular movements.

"Balance of what?" Natalia's eyes were drawn to the steam billowing from the pot behind the old lady.

Baba Yaga turned her head, stood up and poured the liquid into three terracotta cups. The first she carried over to Kuba, setting it down on the bench near his right hand. She caressed his forehead, before walking back and then carrying the other two cups to the table.

"All of it, my girl. I'm here to balance everything," the old woman said. Natalia sipped from the cup, shocked a little by the blend of spices at first, but then finding them warming, comforting. "Remember the lynx outside? Why do you think he didn't run off into the brush? He *knows*. I'm as much a part of what provides order to nature here as the frozen winter winds or the budding of new life in the spring.

"My name isn't *actually* Baba Yaga, either. It was Julia, a long time ago, when I came here, to learn. But the name fits me now. I understand that this is my lot until… until I'm no more and the next Baba Yaga takes my place. And did you notice? No chicken legs beneath my stone cottage either!" She rocked back in her chair, laughing to herself.

Natalia leaned forward over the table. "Why are they so afraid of you? In the village, I mean. Why are they so sure you commune with Satan?"

The old woman's laughter halted. She narrowed her eyes and leaned in close to Natalia. "For a thousand years, people have tended this land. In all that time, there has been someone like me in this cottage, or one like it." She sipped from her tea, her eyes suddenly far away. "But the religion... It doesn't allow for it. Idolatry. Heresy. And so I *must* be Satan's ward. Let me tell you, my girl, there are worse things than your Satan. Old things, older than man, lurking in the shadows and waiting for the balance to tip in their favour."

The lines on Baba Yaga's face seemed to take on a shadow darker than anything else in the old stone cottage. Natalia finished her tea and looked over at her brother, tipping his cup up to drink the last dregs of his own. "We'd best be off, I think. I'll get him settled in and get his temperature up before our mother returns."

The woman stood, gathering the cups and moving them to a shelf at the side of the kitchen. She scooped the rest of the ointment from the mortar into a small clear bottle, then fastened the cap. She handed it over to Natalia.

"Thank you so much, for everything. What can I do to make this up to you? We don't have any money to speak of and the crops are thin at this time of year, but if I can-"

"I require nothing of you other than your secrecy. Keep this bottle well-hidden and mention nothing of your visit here. The village folk might not look kindly upon my… intervention." The old lady walked with Natalia before helping her to heave Kuba back into his barrow, and held the door open and Natalia shoved it out into the frozen forest.

The sun was descending rapidly. She would waste no time getting back to the village.

CHAPTER 5

DOCTOR Malinowski made plain his amazement when he came to check on Kuba's condition ahead of surgery, two days later. The tendrils of the infection which had been creeping their way up Kuba's calf, like sub-dermal poison ivy, had vanished. The rotten smell and pus that had been seeping from the wound were much reduced, the liquid less green and the edges of the newly-formed scar tissue a healthier yellow hue.

He looked up at Natalia. "Have you just been using vodka to clean the wound, as before?" Natalia nodded, saying nothing. "It's remarkable. I've not seen the immune system fight back so effectively without drugs. Not after the infection was so far gone, at least. I'll put off the surgery for a week, to observe his recovery. If it continues at this pace, I'll cancel it altogether." He stood up and ruffled Kuba's sandy hair. "You're doing well young man.

Keep eating whatever these ladies are giving you and you might just keep this leg after all."

He picked up his hat and headed for the door. Natalia looked at Kuba with wide eyes. "What did I tell you, brother?" Kuba grinned back, clearly relieved. "But remember, not a word to Mum, or we'll be in a lot of trouble."

"I *can* tell her what the doctor said, though, right Natka?"

She nodded. "Of course. Now, I'll fix us some lunch." She strode out of the boy's bedroom and into the kitchen.

Natalia watched as her mother smiled for the first time in what felt like months – maybe even years – as Kuba, sitting up in his bed now, the rosy colouration firmly back in his cheeks, recounted the doctor's visit. He unwound the bandage once he finished, proudly showing his mother the leg, looking healthier all the time.

She stepped forward, wrapping her arms around her son's torso, before turning to Natalia and hugging her tightly, thanking her for taking care of him while she'd had to work. Natalia felt a moment of satisfaction that her idea had worked, but more than anything was simply relieved for her brother and glad of a moment's peace from her mother's disappointment.

Days passed with a sense of normalcy from that

moment. Strength returned to Kuba's leg and he was once again able to amble about the house, helping Natalia with the easier chores. There was a single week of his winter break remaining. The snows would soon become intermittent, allowing time for the icy ground to thaw. People would start taking produce to the market again. Life was restarting after its hiatus, as it did every year.

"Natalia, where did we store the excess cotton thread we had last year? After we visited the city with your uncle Adam?"

Natalia was reading a book on her bed, and looked up at her mother, still processing the words of the question mentally. She thought about it for a moment, closing her book after turning down the corner of the page.

"Hmmm… I remember the day," she said, her eyes straining, half-closed as she thought hard. "Oh, I remember, we put it up in the storage cupboard in Kuba's room. The one up in the eaves. Let me get it." She stood, placing her book down on top of the thick woollen blanket.

Her mother's hand stopped her, palm open, pressed against her daughter's chest. "Don't worry, I'll grab it. You're reading. I just have to fix buttons on a couple of the boy's spring shirts. He'll need them before long."

Natalia sat down on the bed and opened her

book again. She glanced outside; Kuba was half-running in the snow with one of the baker's children, unrecognisable from the sickly waif he'd been just days earlier ...

She closed her book and dashed into her brother's room. "Mum, let me-"

"What in hell is this?" Her mother was standing on a wooden step, her face twisted. In her outstretched hand was the tiny jar which had housed Kuba's medicine from Baba Yaga. The lid was off where she'd smelled it, the label handwritten in charcoal, half-text, half-symbol. It was obviously not from the house.

Natalia felt the blood race from her face. "I don't know." She'd tried to say it with confidence, but failed utterly. Her mother stepped down to the floor, reaching forward with the bottle. She placed it into Natalia's hand, closing her fingers around it.

Without warning she slapped Natalia's face, hot and sharp, dizziness causing her to sway from the blow. "That's for lying to me. Now, girl, we'll go to the kitchen and you'll tell me what this is, or that slap will feel like the gentle kiss of an angel."

Natalia paced out of Kuba's room and into the kitchen, her mother's fingers periodically prodding her in the back. She sat at the table, the bottle in her hands, raising it to her nose and smelling the heady fragrances of the honey and spices. She raised her eyes as her mother lowered herself into the chair opposite, her hands balled into fists.

"Speak." A command.

"Kuba's better. His leg's better. Look at him, playing. He's going to be fine, Mum, he's fine."

"Where. Is. It. From?" She reached forward and snatched the bottle from Natalia's hands, holding the smoky glass up to the light of the window, inspecting the last remnants of the viscous liquid that oozed from one side to the other. She shoved the jar back across the table top aggressively. "What are those symbols?"

Natalia picked up the bottle and inspected the symbols, loosely drawn lines of varying densities, forming something that resembled a triangle, a multiple pronged plant, a roughly sketched cylinder. Then writing. Latin, she recognised from school but other languages – if that's what they were – she had no idea of. She shrugged. "I don't know, Mum. I *really* don't."

"Don't lie to me or I'll shut that mouth!" She spat the words, globules of saliva accompanying them, flying forward into Natalia's face. She didn't move, looking terrified at her raging mother as she paused, preparing for her next burst. Then it came. "Tell me this is not from the witch. Tell me this is not the hand of Baba Yaga child. Say it!"

Natalia felt her face redden, her throat grow tight and then the tears begin to escape her blinking eyes. Her whole body shook with the force of her weeping, still not conscious of what was really happening as her mother stood and walked past her.

Then came the feeling of rough hands tugging at her long blonde hair and dragging her backward, tipping her almost over the back of her chair. Out of the kitchen to the door. Her mother tugged back the door, the small jar tucked into her over shirt. The wind hit Natalia, dressed in her long skirt and a jumper, like a hammer of ice.

She staggered under the force of her mother's dragging, dropping to her knees, the frozen snow and frost biting at her skin, then standing again. She looked back to the house, and the distant figures of Kuba and his friend outside. She tried to cry out but found no voice. Then she looked once more at her mother, her face full of fear and rage and hate.

"It's the church for you, girl. Let our Lord pass his judgement for what you've done to that poor, innocent boy."

Beyond her raging mother, the austere grey of the church tower was a single dark finger raised in warning against the bright winter sky.

Father Mateusz was a stern man, in his seventies. He had served in the war and still had the limp to show for it. Natalia knew him well enough from Sunday school and knew, too, that he was not one to look kindly upon transgressions from his devout interpretation of the faith.

She perched on the edge of the hard chair opposite him as he paced up and down behind his desk, clutching the small jar in his hand. She could feel the heat as her face swelled where her mother had struck her. Her mother had revealed everything – including the miraculous nature of Kuba's recovery – and then the priest had gone quiet, forcibly seating Natalia and walking back and forth. Silent.

Finally, he sat.

"You have lived in this parish your entire life, Natalia. Is that not correct?"

Natalia looked directly at the priest and nodded.

"Have you not been educated in the teachings of Christ, and taught – painstakingly at times – to tread the path that leads you away from the temptation to consort with Satan?"

"I have, Father. But Kuba's leg – there was no medicine, he was going to be crippled-"

"You would sell your soul to the King of Hell in exchange for your brother's ability to walk?" The priest stood and paced again. His eyes met those of Natalia's mother and they each shook their heads. "Don't ignore my question girl!" He barked the sentence from across the room.

"The witch – Baba Yaga – is not Satan. She worships nature and she made medicine. I didn't sell anything to anyone. She just wanted to help me, to help Kuba." As she finished speaking she looked down at her hands, fidgeting with them in her lap. She felt the presence of Father Mateusz standing over her.

"*Even Satan disguises himself as an angel of light.* Do you remember these words, Natalia?"

She looked up at the priest, his haggard face looming over her, outrage burning in his eyes. She nodded. "Two Corinthians, isn't it?"

"You know, and yet you let this woman, this servant of the below, deceive you." He walked back away, sitting again behind his desk. He pulled out a drawer and a sheaf of paper which he placed on the desk in front of him. He unscrewed the cap of a fountain pen and began to write. Then he stopped, the nib hovering over the page like a hawk waiting to swoop at its prey. He looked up at Natalia's mother. "The girl will be punished, but I am unauthorised to preside over such things. The decision will be made by the bishop. His response will take a few days." Fixing his gaze on Natalia, he went on. "We will examine your brother for signs of contamination. Let us hope for your sake that he is not host to anything demonic. In the meantime, you are to say one hundred and twenty *Hail Mary's* each night before bed, so that the Lord's mercy might be bestowed upon you."

Natalia nodded, still not looking up at the priest. Her mother's hand on her shoulder was her cue to stand. She turned and walked towards the door.

Then the priest called out to her. "Natalia." She spun around, her head swimming. "I do not want to hear of any such thing again or I cannot guarantee your safety. Do you understand?"

She nodded again. "Thank you, Father." They left the church and walked back across the snowy field towards home, not a word passing between them.

CHAPTER 6

THE SNOWS had abated overnight. The white blanket that had muffled the world for the past two months and more was growing patchy outside Natalia's bedroom window. Six days had passed since the encounter with Father Mateusz and as each day passed without action – without punishment – she could feel her anxiety receding.

"Good morning," her mother said to her as she ambled out of her room, rubbing the sleep from her eyes. "I made toast and eggs. Come on."

Natalia put her arms by her sides and followed her mother into the kitchen. It was the first time they'd spoken in anything resembling a normal way since the discovery of the jar. A plate of scrambled eggs and toast was waiting for her, the fluffy yellow and white eggs topped with sliced chives. Natalia's favourite since early childhood.

"Did someone say eggs?" Kuba walked in to the

kitchen, swaying, still entranced with sleep.

Natalia turned to him, smiling. "He must be getting better if his stomach wakes him up in the morning."

Kuba poked his tongue at her and sat down, his mother placing another slice of bread under the grill and turning the flame back on under the remaining eggs. She served him his portion within a few minutes and sat, watching her children.

"Thanks for this, Mum. It's delicious." Natalia tasted the butter the eggs had been cooked in, deliciously fatty in such icy weather.

"It's a wonderful day, for both of you." She lifted a forkful of toast and egg into her mouth and chewed, taking a sip from her tea to wash it down. She placed the cup back down on the table. "Father Mateusz came today, at dawn."

Natalia dropped her fork, which clattered loudly against the plate. She stared at her mother, waiting for her to go on.

"He says you'll not be punished, either of you. In the circumstances, the bishop has seen fit to forgive you your transgression and has come to the village to offer a blessing to the two of you. To purify you both after what happened."

Natalia picked up her fork and started stabbing at her bread with it. "On a Thursday? Has the bishop even *been* here before?" She heaped another forkful into her mouth and chewed.

"Of course he has! Well, not this one, but his

predecessor came to inaugurate our church when it was reconstructed after the war. Anyway, he's here for you today, so I've managed to take the day off of work – one of the other girls is covering for me – and we're leaving in an hour."

Natalia focussed on her food, unresponsive. She looked at Kuba. "Do you want to go?" Her brother nodded, pouring himself water from the steel jug on the table. Natalia sighed and then looked back to her mother. "How long is this blessing going to take?"

Her mother stood and carried her plate over to the sink and began rinsing it. "Well, that's what the breakfast is for. The priest said you'd need a full stomach and it might be a long day."

"Great." Natalia said the word precisely and without enthusiasm. She stood and took her own plate to the sink to clean.

"You have to be ready, Natka. One hour. I've laid formal clothes out for you on the chest at the end of my bed. You want to look your best." Her mother dashed into the bathroom, humming.

"Of course," said Natalia, tugging off her robe as she shut the door.

The three of them trudged through the melting snow from their small holding at one end of the village, all the way to the church at the other. Kuba leaned on the stick that Natalia had found him, gripping his big sister's hand with the other. Their mother walked a few paces ahead of the children, mumbling to herself.

As they came around to the village square, Natalia felt the hair on the back of her neck stand on end. Everyone was there – the family who ran the bakery, the butcher and his wife, the post master. *Everyone*. The bishop stood outside, a thick grey cape over his white robes. His mitre hat, in pristine white, inlaid with opulent gold, stood out like a crown. As they approached, he opened his arms and stepped forward to hold their mother in a tight embrace, whispering into her ear. She knelt in front of him as he released her, crossing herself.

Natalia stepped forward, kneeling and making the sign of the cross. The bishop drew a cross in the air with this right hand and welcomed her to the church. Kuba did the same, without kneeling because of his injury. They were led in to the church and shown by Father Mateusz to two seats, close to the altar. Their mother sat back among the congregation, in the third row. Natalia looked back at her and thought she detected discomfort in the smile that she supposed was intended to reassure her.

She swallowed hard and turned to face the front just as the organ music held a chord and then went quiet. The bishop stepped forward to the lectern and began to speak. The Latin Mass. Natalia had studied Latin in school for two years. She knew how to conjugate the most basic of verbs but little more. As ever, this service would fly over her head, meaninglessly. She looked at her little brother, his eyes darting all over the inside of the church from one gilded portrait of Christ or the Holy Mother to the next. She imagined how much worse it must have been for him. They sat and at least pretended to pay attention, standing at the appropriate moments to join in with hymns and prayers which, mercifully, were in their own language. The service ended, as ever, with the standing and the offering of peace to one's neighbours. Natalia stood and stepped back to the front row of pews, exchanging handshakes and kisses on the cheek with the village residents there, including her mother, then she was coaxed back to the front by the priest. The bishop wasn't yet finished.

"One and all, you well know that we are gathered in this place today to offer a blessing to these children of the Lord who, in their naivety, accepted help from one allied to the fallen one. And, as is written in the holy scripture, the gifts bestowed by Satan are not empty. See how the boy's leg has recovered. Stand, Jakub, stand." The bishop ushered him to his feet with a wave of his arm, his robes gathering and adding further drama to the scene.

Kuba stood, still leaning heavily on the length of wood. A murmur went around the congregation that rose from a whisper to a buzz in a matter of moments. "Silence," Father Mateusz called out from the side of the bishop. And there was silence, but for the shuffling of bodies on the hardwood pews.

"Sit, boy," said the bishop in a calmer tone. Kuba sat. "So you see that the gifts of the dark one are not to be avoided because they are false but because his *promises* are false. It is for this reason that we must bless these children today, to reaffirm the vows that you, the community made on their behalf at their baptisms, years ago. But it is for this reason, too, that they must confess their sins and atone."

The murmur rose again, until the bishop's voice once again sliced through it.

"Do you confess your sins, of commune with a representative of the devil in exchange for the gift of your brother's mobility?" He looked into Natalia's eyes, unblinking. She felt her muscles begin to tremble, the echo of the bishop's words still bouncing around the wide space of the church. She could sense the community staring daggers into her back.

The prodigal. The sinner.

She thought for a moment about arguing her case. She knew all too well that Baba Yaga had no pact with Satan. Indeed, she doubted even the existence of this cartoonish prince of darkness whose portrait was so lavishly painted and imbued with villainy in the good book. But she thought better of it. If this was the sideshow they needed to move past this without any great upheaval, let them have it. She nodded. "I do, your holiness. I confess to everything of which I stand accused."

The bishop nodded and turned his head to Kuba, preaching a near-identical mantra of castigation. Kuba didn't seem to pause to think at all, simply following his older sister's lead, nodding and confessing. It was over. They had sat through the Mass, the blessing and now they had confessed their sins to the highest representative of the Vatican in the region. Natalia shuffled in her seat, anxious to leave.

"Now then, in order that no such innocent children might be moved to act in such a foolish way, nor to tread such a path fraught with peril again, we as a community will follow the young ones into the forest and we shall dispose of this servant of the abyss together."

A cry rose from the back of the room and the hum of conversation rose and rose until it was a meaningless, near deafening babble. Natalia spun around, looking at the people, all now clutching wooden stakes and other tools and weapons that had been out of sight when she arrived. Parishioners were filing out of the building in an ordered line, into the crisp late-winter air. She looked back at the bishop, her mouth agape with terror. "What's happening?"

"We are going to rid ourselves of that filthy witch and you are going to show us the way," the bishop said, his voice seemingly free of any emotion.

Natalia began to feel beads of sweat forming under her clothes. She shuffled in her chair. "Unless you seek to protect the one who led you away from the true path?" The bishop's voice boomed through the near-empty church.

Natalia looked up at him, his stern expression unflinching. She felt herself tremble.

The bishop's features softened to a smile and he motioned the two of them towards the doors at the rear of the church. "Come then," he said. "Let us all pay a visit to your witch." He waited for them to stand and began to follow them out of the church, his footsteps percussive, reverberating off the high walls.

Outside they were greeted with a hive of energy, people milling to and fro, laughing and calling out to one another. The snow underfoot had been trodden down to a grey slush, squelching noisily as people moved. The men carried sticks, sledgehammers, lengths of rope and Piotr, the pub owner, carried a small barrel, liquid sloshing around inside.

Kuba looked up at Natalia, fear turning his face pale. "What's happening, Natka? What are they going to do with Baba Yaga?"

She looked down at her little brother, walking with the aid of his long wooden support. "I think you should go home. I don't want you to see, whatever it is." She looked across to her mother, her eyes pleading. "Mum, take him home. He doesn't need to be a part of this."

Their mother looked at the boy, hobbling with his stick, real anguish in her eyes. But then she looked up towards the bishop, approaching from behind Natalia, and shook her head. "There's no other way. They said... no other way."

Natalia spun around and looked at the bishop, then at Father Mateusz as he joined them after locking the church doors. Their expressions were stern, unmoved.

"Are you going to make my brother watch? He's ten years old." She spoke quietly, holding Kuba close and turning his face away from the scene.

Father Mateusz opened his mouth to speak but the bishop raised his hand, silencing him. "I was of the opinion that we had made the severity of your transgression quite clear," he said, his intonation flat, without any detectable emotion.

"Then punish *me*. I took him there, I knew the way, I asked for help. He was led into all of this by me. I don't want him to be damaged because of *my* decision. He's a little boy."

The bishop brought his cloaked hand up to his chin, pausing and talking to himself under his breath. Then he fixed his eyes on Natalia's. "My dear child, let me assure you that nothing deepens a young person's attachment to God quite like an indescribable fear of the alternative. Now get to the front of this group. You will lead the way." He looked down at Kuba, whose eyes were wide with fear. "And worry not, I'll ensure your brother has an unobscured view."

CHAPTER 7

THE SUN was high in the sky, creating skeletal shadows of naked branches on the forest floor, when they reached the old woman's house. She was standing, alone, on the porch, seemingly waiting for them.

Natalia felt her eyes well with tears as she saw her. She carefully mouthed the words 'I'm sorry.' Baba Yaga looked at her and smiled, bringing her hands together as if in prayer. She closed her eyes and bowed her head toward Natalia.

"Is this the woman?" The voice of the bishop was gravelly, harsh.

Natalia nodded, eyes closed, tears tracing lines down her face. She opened them again and watched as the interrogation began.

"Are you the one that calls yourself Baba Yaga?"

The old woman returned her hands to her sides. She took a deep breath in and began. "I am not the one that uses this name, but it is the name that others use of me, yes."

"Very well, *Baba Yaga*, did you not perform witchcraft, using power granted to you by your unholy communion with Lucifer, to heal this boy?"

The mob of people started jeering, words and hisses mingling into a wall of white noise. Kuba went to his sister's side, burying his face in her torso. Natalia put her hand on the back of his head and rubbed at his hair.

Baba Yaga was smiling, a broad grin of amusement. "If you must know, your holiness, I used honey, cinnamon bark and peppermint. To my knowledge, none of those comes from Lucifer."

The postmaster stepped forward, striking her across the face with his gloved hand. "You'll not speak to the bishop in that tone."

"Thank you, but that won't be necessary" the bishop said, urging the man back into the crowd. "I will consider your protests when I pass judgement. Myself and Father Mateusz will come into the cottage now and search for evidence of demonic influence. Do you object?"

She looked at the bishop, the smile on her face receding. "If you must," she said, and stepped away from the door. The two men walked inside and the sounds of benches being moved along the stone floor and glass vials being scattered and smashed emanated from the open door.

Natalia approached. She stared at her own hands

and then glanced up at Baba Yaga. "It was an accident – people finding out, I mean. I kept the bottle in a high, hidden place, I didn't want anyone to know. I'm so sorry."

Baba Yaga looked her in the eye. "Child, none of this is your doing. I knew the risk I was taking when I helped you. I'm just glad that you're going to be safe. Now go to your brother, he looks terrified."

Natalia nodded and scampered back, embracing Kuba. She turned around to see the two holy men walking out of the stone house. The bishop was clutching a handful of bottles, while Father Mateusz had a wooden cage with a jackdaw sitting inside.

"Like the one the girl had, each of these vials contains a queer substance and each of them is labelled with a script I do not recognise and symbols that do not appear wholesome!" The bishop's voice boomed dramatically, silencing the villagers. "And look to Father Mateusz, the witch's familiar – a crow!" The buzz of conversation rose again to a near deafening level. The bishop looked from one side of the crowd to the other. The villagers' expressions had hardened and cries of 'witch' and 'heretic' could be heard.

Father Mateusz raised his hand. "Hush now, everyone. Hush." Silence returned to the woods. "What do you say to these accusations, madam?" He fixed her with his eyes.

She reached out a hand, taking the cage from him by its handle. She put a finger through the bars, caressing the bird's short, angular beak. "This is a jackdaw, not a crow. And the reason she is in this cage is that her wing was broken. You can see the splint I made her, here." She held the cage aloft, showing it to the mob and sending them into a whispering frenzy.

The bishop was not to be deterred. He placed the bottles in a pouch at the front of his robes and stepped forward. "Helping it or otherwise, do any of you have a connection so close with a wild animal of the forest? See how she lavishes attention on it as we would our dogs or cattle? This can be no mere savage carrion bird. It acts as her eyes and ears, and we can be sure that, when its wing is repaired, those beady eyes will be upon you, the village folk, spying."

The people started chattering again, their voices growing louder and louder to the point of cacophony. Natalia watched as the bishop's face changed to one of delight. He raised both hands above his head this time, urging quiet once more. After a time, the people acquiesced.

"Baba Yaga," he said, more quietly, laden with less spite. "You stand accused of commune with the devil, of witchcraft and of corrupting two minors into the ways of Satan. Is there anything you would like to say in your defence?"

Baba Yaga let her wild hair down from behind her head. She looked out at the people in front of her without saying a word, then she spoke. "I have lived in these woods for nearly fifty years, and before me there has been someone with the title of Baba Yaga for close to a millennium. Many of you standing here today have visited this place for cures, advice and treatment. I have told you all the same thing. I do not serve your God, your Lord. I serve something older, the very essence of nature – the spirit of the wilderness. More than that, I stand as intermediary between man and the savage world. I have long awaited the day when you would strike me down and I will tell you what the last woman in my place told me. He who strikes me down shall awaken the untamed, shall unbridle that over which man claims dominion and shall ultimately be held responsible for their actions."

A hush fell over the villagers. The sound of branches snapping in the surrounding bushes startled those nearest to them.

The bishop took a step towards Baba Yaga, his hand outstretched. "These are not the dark ages. We must burn your property, but we will not execute you. You will be imprisoned." He nodded towards the pub owner.

Piotr marched forward, pulling the cork from the barrel he carried, and began to spray liquid around the walls of the building. He walked inside, continuing to douse everything, the fragrance of petrol harsh in Natalia's throat in the chafing winter air.

Baba Yaga walked up to the bishop, holding the

caged jackdaw by her side. She pressed her nose against his and spoke coldly, unblinking. "I *am* all that there is inside that house. If my cottage is to be consumed by fire, then so shall I."

The bishop swallowed audibly, the breeze suddenly hushed in this open pocket of the forest. "Very well," he said, his voice quivering. He glanced toward Natalia and her brother and then back at Baba Yaga as she disappeared into the old cottage.

The pub owner stepped out onto the doorstep, looking confused, his barrel now empty. His eyes searched those of the bishop, of Father Mateusz, then of Natalia. He looked back as the door closed firmly. Then the first candles inside found the fuel.

With a rush that sounded like a thousand sharp breaths in unison, a flame of blue and yellow and gold enveloped the house, searching for wood and moss and fabric to take hold of and to ignite. The sound of glass expanding and shattering punctuated the silence that emanated eerily from the inside of the house.

Then a faint tune drifted out through the open window. First it was just humming, a tune that no one knew, but Natalia could tell from the faces as they all stopped, tuned completely to it, that it was somehow familiar to them. Then the lyrics crept out, the old woman's voice withering as the smoke and flames choked it out. But they all heard it. They all heard the words.

Be silent, my children, can't you hear?
The wilderness spirit chimes a warning call.
Be silent, my children, but do not fear,
The final reckoning awaits us all.
Nature's great forces, love and wrath.
Be careful my children, as you choose your path.

As the last lines rang out from the window, the sound of the voice began to tremble and then quieted to a hiss. She didn't scream. Didn't protest or beg for mercy.

Kuba had attached himself to Natalia's legs. She could feel his hands clutching at her clothing and was relieved to see that his eyes were scrunched shut when she looked down at him. She looked back up just in time to see two of the wooden beams in the roof collapse, uneven panels of slate tumbling noisily into the blaze.

She turned to the bishop. "It's over. Can we go home now?" She could see her mother out of the corner of her eye, making placating gestures, silently telling her to calm down. But she would not. They had just watched an innocent woman burn. She herself had been responsible for it and her brother had been forced to witness it. She was seething.

The bishop looked at her at an angle. He smiled and said, "You need to learn to respect your betters, girl. But yes, the old crone is gone and with her, her black magic. I don't suppose you'll get up to any mischief beyond the usual for a girl your age. You can take your brother and get out of-"

He was interrupted by the injured jackdaw flying up from the hole in the roof, cawing noisily. It sat on a damaged beam, smoke clouding around it against the pale grey sky. It called out again, its voice gravelly and harsh, before turning its head from side to side and then shaking its body and wings, becoming a monochrome blur. The splint and bindings flung free, it flew up into the air, then swooped directly toward the bishop, knocking his pointed hat to the ground. It perched for a moment in a tree, eyeing the villagers as they stood in silent shock. Then it frantically flapped its wings once more and launched itself, its beak and clawed feet slashing at the bishop's face and neck.

He held up his arms, droplets of blood tainting his pure white robes as the bird struck at him again and again, until the hulking pub owner swung at it with an iron poker. The bird was flung across the clearing, shattered, its wings quivering as it lay dying on the ground.

Father Mateusz immediately ran to the bishop's side, bending to look at the lacerations that ran from just below his left eye to his neck. "We'll need to get some iodine on that. It cut you quite deeply."

The bishop shoved him away and stood tall, straightening his robes and replacing his hat, after Piotr had returned it to him. "It's nothing serious, I'm sure, but I'll patch it up in your office before returning to the city. Now let's get away from this festering hole." He started walking without looking back.

Natalia watched all of this unfold and then looked back at the villagers, many of them with hands over open mouths.

They had heard the song – indeed many of them had likely visited Baba Yaga themselves. They knew that she was tied to the wild things in the forest in ways that none of them fully understood, and fear was now written large on all of their faces. They began to walk silently away from the clearing, the cracking of their boots on old twigs like echoes of the snapping of objects ignited in the fire behind them.

Natalia held her brother close to her as they both looked down at the jackdaw, lying on its side in a patch of half-melted snow. They watched silently, waiting until it stopped twitching. Dead. Their eyes met and they followed the village folk out of the forest.

CHAPTER 8

Over the forty-eight hours that followed, what had happened in the forest was forcibly ignored. With the snow melting, and the first life of spring evident on the trees and in the grasses that were sprouting up, Natalia spent more time in the village, trading jars of preserved fruit and vegetables that her mother had made, and coming back with butter, goat's cheese, bread and even a blood pudding sausage from the butcher. Every exchange was pregnant with the horrors they had all witnessed as a community, but no one would talk about it. Eye contact came at a premium, while smiles were worn clumsily, forced, an unspoken admission of fear and pain.

The bishop had returned to the city that same day, unlikely to be seen in the village again, his work – the great show of the power of the church – already complete. Now it was the villagers who were left to deal with the actions they had taken together. The weight of the guilt weighed on no one more heavily than Natalia.

Her errands complete and her mother at work, she decided it was time to visit the house in the forest once more. To pay her respects and ask forgiveness.

It was early afternoon when she set out, making far swifter progress with the snow all but gone. Dazzling sunlight beat down on her and she had to unfasten her jacket as her quick pace meant she built up quite a sweat. At the edge of the forest she detected a sweet fragrance and looked up to see life was busily restarting after its annual hiatus. Buds were forming on branches where birds sat and chirped loudly. They flitted one way and the other, flying close together in play. As ever in this part of the woods, shadows moved in her peripheral vision, and she remained uncertain of whether these were animals, figments of her imagination or the old forces that Baba Yaga had channelled in her craft. Unperturbed, she hurried on to where the old stone cottage stood.

Her mouth hung wide open as she saw the house. The patches of moss that had lent the place its antique quality had expanded, now carpeting the ill-matched stones that made up the walls. Crisscrossed over the top were lines of ivy, woven in all directions, the entire façade of the house a shimmering palette of gleaming greens. How was it possible in just two days? The door to the house was impassable, overgrown too with the moss and ivy, thick golden fungus sprouting from its edges.

Natalia took a step back and felt something crunch beneath her feet. She spun around to see the jackdaw, its body stripped completely of feathers and flesh, an almost surgically clean skeleton with two tiny black beetles scouring the bones for anything that was left to devour.

She closed her eyes. This was wrong.

Picking up her pace, she dashed to the rear of the house where she prised open a heavily burnt wooden window frame. Light streamed in through the holes in the roof, revealing a floor awash with ferns, brambles and bushes. Baba Yaga's body was nowhere to be seen, doubtless deep beneath all the plant matter. She pulled harder at the window, bending the damaged hinges until the wood began to splinter and then snapped. She leaned the broken window panel against the wall of the cottage and lifted herself up to the window, her head and half of her torso inside the building. The smell of burning and of the fuel lingered, but they were background scents. The pervading fragrance was one of sweetness, of chlorophyll, of *life*.

"I don't really even know why I'm here," she said, as her eyes scanned for Baba Yaga's body. "I just wanted you to know that what happened was never what I had intended. And that I'm sorry that I wasn't more careful with the bottle. And that I didn't fight them harder. To prevent all this."

Her body quaked as she sobbed at the futility of her confession, tears cascading over her cheeks. Then she felt a presence. Someone watching her. She looked around the inside of the house but found nothing. She lowered herself to the ground and spun around, seeing only more shadows flinching and scurrying away in the thickets that surrounded the old building.

Then she turned to her left and saw the lynx. Its eyes were wide, the black pupils dilated, only a sliver of iridescent yellow surrounding them. It stepped towards her, paws placed silently and deliberately with every motion. Natalia took in a deep breath and held it, her body beginning to tremble involuntarily. Then it was next to her, blood matted into the fur of its heavy, clawed paws and steam rising from its slightly open mouth as it panted.

The lynx lurched forward, its wet nose making contact with Natalia's tear-streaked cheek. It opened its mouth wider, canine teeth long, sharp weapons. It tilted its head to one side, licking the tears from her cheek and then nuzzled her, the tufts at the side of its face warm against her skin. It pulled back and then butted against her, its big eyes now closed, floppy ears folding back as it rubbed its head on hers.

Natalia slowly raised her right hand and placed it at the back of the animal's strong neck and began to rub it back and forth. The lynx stepped a little closer, as if it were a gigantic housecat. A handful of minutes passed before the lynx stepped back, sitting on its hind legs and cleaning its face. When it was finished, it stood at full height, leaned forward, its face close to the ground, stretching, then stood back up. It looked into Natalia's eyes, blinked, and then turned and disappeared into the forest, no more than a flying shadow.

Natalia held her hand to her chest and leaned against the wall, her breath quick and heavy. Once she had caught her breath, she sped from the forest and returned home.

CHAPTER 9

HER MOTHER woke her earlier than usual the next morning, dragging her violently from a vivid dream about the forest and the encounter with the lynx. Startled, she sat up abruptly. "What's the matter, Mum? What time is it?" she said. Almost no light was creeping into the room from the cracks around the curtains.

"It's the church, Natalia." Her mother was pacing back and forth in the room as she spoke, her voice jittery. "I woke up this morning before six and something wouldn't let me go back to sleep. I had this feeling that just wouldn't go away." She stopped pacing and sat down on her own bed, opposite Natalia's.

"Fine, Mum, but what does it have to do with the church?"

Her mother stood again at the question and walked to the chest of drawers that contained many of Natalia's clothes. She began tugging out underwear, socks, a vest and a top that her daughter could wear for the day. When she'd finished she stayed facing away from her daughter.

"When I couldn't sleep again, I had an urge. To go and pray, you know? I think a lot of us in the village have been wondering if what we did was right. The other day in the forest, I mean." Natalia nodded and sounded her agreement without words, waiting for her mother to continue. "Well, when I got there ... Nothing could have prepared me." She turned and looked at Natalia, placing the clothes she'd taken from the chest on the end of her bed.

"What was it, Mum, what did you see?" Natalia pulled back the blanket on the bed and turned her body to get up, her feet searching for her slippers, so as to avoid the icy cold floor. She stood up, picking up the clothes her mum had selected. Her mother looked away again.

"Get dressed, Natka. It's best you see for yourself. I'll give you a minute." She scurried out of the room without another word, closing the door behind her.

Natalia stood and quickly dressed, opening the wardrobe to fish out a heavy overshirt to protect her from the wintry winds that still blew across the plains, even as spring was bedding in. She opened the door when she was dressed, still running a stiff brush through her tangled hair.

"Should I get Kuba out of bed, Mum?" she called through to the kitchen.

Her mother dashed out to meet her then, a finger of warning held vertical over her lips. "Don't wake the boy. He's been through enough. He's better off here, warm and resting."

Natalia had no reason to argue with her mother's logic, so she pulled down her coat and scarf, wrapping herself up before she and her mother ventured into the dawn light.

She fought the urge to ask for more information on the way to the village, her mother clearly spooked by whatever she had found. Instead Natalia took the opportunity to listen to the daybreak songs of starlings and finches in the scrabbly clumps of trees that dotted the path. She made certain to look away from the forest as they passed, not yet ready to face her visit from yesterday, neither in reality, nor her imagination.

As they came to the bakery that marked the start of the town proper, Natalia could see something was somehow wrong at the church. The dark stone was almost impossible to focus on in the dim light, while the sun was still valiantly attempting to scale the horizon, but she was sure she could see motion. The church seemed alive, teeming with... something.

Desperate to see what, she quickened her pace, her mother keeping up with her as best she could. With about fifty metres to go, she stopped. It was clear now, the walls were covered with insects, spiders and grubs. A shroud of living creatures crawling in all directions, stepping over one another and transforming the dark brown brick into the shiny black of their legs and wing cases. The arched wooden door, too, had not been left unscathed. Along the bottom edge of the door were a series of roughly cut holes, about five centimetres tall.

They walked towards the old building, driven on by curiosity but slowed by fear and revulsion, their eyes drawn ceaselessly to the writhing shapes that littered the walls. The door stood ajar, the wrought iron handle coming away from the partially consumed wood. Natalia was unable to take her eyes from the melee of creatures less than a metre above her head as she shoved the door forward. It creaked loudly, the high-pitched whine cutting sharply through the silence of the sleeping world.

Inside was worse. Rats and mice of myriad sizes and colours ran in all directions, climbing, as with the bugs outside, over one another and eating away at everything. Pews were missing corners and edges. Prayer cushions were founts of errant stuffing, their coverings devoured. Three mice clung to the large wooden cross suspended above the altar, already eating both into the substance of the crucifix itself, as well as the wooden figure of Christ suspended from it. Natalia's mother dropped almost to her knee – she was loath to touch the ground and the plague of rodents – and crossed herself. Natalia watched her, but felt no compulsion to follow suit.

At once she had a thought and whispered to her mother. "Where's Father Mateusz? Isn't the vicarage adjoined to the church building?"

Her mother's mouth opened as if to speak, but found herself unable to respond. Her lips moved silently and then she sealed them, nodded and flicked her head towards the door behind the altar and the suspended tubes of the wooden organ. Natalia sped ahead, trying not to tread on the scurrying mice, unsure if this was out of a will to avoid harming them or from pure disgust.

She shoved at the door. As with the one at the front of the church, it gave, the lock eaten away. The door opened onto a hallway, from which there were three doors. Natalia turned the handle on to the nearest one and found a small sitting room. Two old couches sat at right angles facing an antique-looking sideboard equipped with a radio and a gramophone. There was no sign of the infestation here and Natalia felt her thundering heart slow at this discovery. On a low coffee table sat a battered old copy of the Bible, in Latin by the looks of it, with dog-eared notes stuffed higgledy-piggledy between the pages. Natalia crouched beside the book and flicked through, her lack of Latin scholarship obscuring what she was looking at, save for the untidy, handwritten scribbles in her own language. She stood as her mother called out

"Father! Father Mateusz! Are you in here?"

Silence.

Natalia joined in, walking up the corridor and crying out shrilly "Father! It's Natalia! Are you here?!"

A thumping sound came from the end of the hall. Natalia eyed her mother, whose expression had completely frozen over. She mouthed words to her. *'Did you hear that?'* Her mother simply nodded again, still seemingly dumbstruck by the situation. They edged up the hallway to where there were two more doors, one opposite the other. The door to the left was ajar. Natalia's mother pushed it gently and it swung open.

Still.

Silent.

Empty.

They stepped inside the room, drawing back the curtain over the old enamel bath, and saw a single, fat cockroach circling the plug hole, the hairs on its legs sticking out at odd angles, its antennae probing the droplets of water in front of it. They turned and crept out of the room. Natalia looked up to her mother and then knocked hard with the knuckles of her right hand.

A muffled vocal sound and three more thumps came from the room. She looked into her mother's eyes once more and turned the handles, shoving the door inward. She stepped into the room and began to choke. Father Mateusz was stretched out on the bed, a sea of oversized ants, beetles and flying insects writhing and buzzing over his body. He tried to call out but a wave of insects rushed into his mouth and down his throat, muffling the sound.

Natalia stood paralysed, her hands absent-mindedly covering her mouth.

She wrenched her eyes from the sight on the bed to her mother, who said a single word. "Water."

Natalia understood and burst back into the bathroom. She looked around for something, any kind of container to transport water in. There was nothing in the bath or on any of the shelves. She knelt in front of the basin and opened the cupboard. There was a bowl. It couldn't have held more than about a litre, but it would have to do. She grasped it and threw it in to the sink, turning on the tap to its full flow.

"Hurry, Natalia!" her mother called from across the hallway.

When the water started to flow over the rounded edge, she grasped the bowl with both hands and hurried from the bathroom, water sloshing onto the floor as she half-ran into the room.

Her mother stepped aside, offering instructions. "His head first Natka, go on."

She looked up to her mother in acknowledgement and then emptied the bowl over the priest's head, insects scattering in all directions with the flow of the liquid. Natalia stopped for a moment and stared at Father Mateusz's face, his skin raw and eaten away around his eyes and mouth, one of his cheeks torn right through.

"Get more, Natka! We need to get him out of here!" Her mother was yelled in her ear, waking

Natalia from her malaise.

She turned and dashed back into the bathroom, filling the basin again and returning. As she jogged back into the bedroom, her mother was swiping aside insects that were moving onto the priest's head again with her forearm, cursing as they bit and stung her. Natalia threw the next pot of water over the man's shoulders and upper torso. Her mother clutched his arm and started trying to drag him from the bed.

She turned to her daughter as she tried to heave his weight up. "One more should do it, just to get them off his legs, yes?"

Natalia nodded and ran out again. She came back and doused his legs and midriff with the last bowlful and then threw it onto the floor, taking Father Mateusz's other arm and dragging him off the bed. His pyjamas were shredded and blood soaked, sores and gashes running the length of his entire body. Natalia tried not to stare as they dragged him from the room, but couldn't help herself as the final few creatures belligerently clung to their prey, biting and secreting burning, acidic saliva.

As they exited the room, Father Mateusz tried to talk, his tongue, too, a tapestry of cuts and swollen sores. He tugged at Natalia's arm as he framed the words. "This way. The back door."

They dragged him around the corner at the end of the corridor, behind the bathroom door and to a door. The priest leaned against the wall, Natalia having let go of him to open the catch on the door. She swung it open and went back to him for support, before dragging him out into the fresh morning air. They lowered him to the dewy grass and sat beside him, the exhaustion of the situation now beginning to show its effects. They watched the teeming life on the rear wall of the church and vicarage in silence for a few moments, their breath heavy and fast.

Natalia spoke first. "Stay with him, Mum. I'll get Doctor Malinowski." She pushed herself up from the ground with her hands with no small amount of effort and walked the short distance to Malinowski's cottage. She banged on the door. No response. She looked up at the sky – it couldn't be eight in the morning yet, judging by the light. She banged again and heard shuffling inside the house.

At last the door opened. The doctor's smile looked forced. "Natalia, good morning, child. What can I do for you?" He was wearing thick towelling pyjamas and a robe, his hair standing on end in all directions. He yawned and rubbed sleep from his eyes.

"You must be sick of seeing me, Doctor. But it's Father Mateusz. He's cut all over, bleeding and I don't know what to do. Will you come?" She felt her heart begin to beat faster in her chest. She swallowed.

"Of course I'll come. Where is he? And how did

this happen?" The doctor turned around, looking for his leather bag and finding it beneath the coat stand. "Come inside while I dress; you can explain through the door." He beckoned her into the cottage.

Natalia followed him and stood outside in the hallway while the doctor changed his clothes in the bedroom. "He was covered in insects, and things, Doctor. They were all over him. When me and Mum found him, they'd eaten through his bedsheets and his pyjamas. They were even inside his mouth, biting his tongue. I think he might have swallowed some. I don't... oh my God, I just... I don't know."

The doctor rushed out of the room, still tucking his unironed shirt into his trousers. "Insects? Where was this, the vicarage?" he said. Natalia nodded. "But it's a stone building. How did they...? I mean, I know we all have a few ants and beetles in the summer − spiders in the autumn, too − but this makes no sense. Are you quite sure, Natalia?"

"It's the witch, Doctor. Baba Yaga. This all started after she was put to death. And at her house. There's... everything's strange. Not as it should be. But we've got no time. Father Mateusz might not survive if we don't go now."

The doctor nodded and went to pick up his bag. He opened it and began inspecting the contents, then he turned to Natalia. "If he's cut we'll need bandages. Go to the high cupboard in my bathroom, bring as much as you can find. I'm just going to go to my office and get some sedatives and pain killers."

"Top cupboard, right." Natalia ran to the bathroom. Within a minute they were both ready to go.

The doctor reached up to the coat rack and pulled down an old jacket and scarf and handed them to Natalia. "You must be freezing. Get that wet coat off and use this one."

She thanked him, switched coats and they left for the church. Natalia tried to balance her pace between the urgency she felt and respectful acknowledgement of the doctor's old age and reduced mobility. She caught herself edging away a little too far in front more than once and fell back. "Can I carry your bag, Doctor?"

The old man shook his head. "No, no. No need. And it's my legs slowing me down, not the weight, believe me, Natalia."

She nodded and managed a smile in acceptance. The short few minutes passed as though an agonising eternity for her, but they arrived before long. Father Mateusz was draped in a blanket that her mother had scavenged from somewhere. His face was a bloody wreck, more striking than she'd first thought now that the blood had been wiped away. His bottom lip was virtually non-existent, hanging gorily away from his jaw. When he opened his mouth to try to speak, his tongue was a vivid red that was part bloody wound and part swollen bite or sting. Natalia read the visible shock in the doctor's face.

"What happened?" The old man asked the question to no one in particular as he crouched, opening his bag and pulling out various pieces of equipment. He passed a couple of objects to Natalia to hold as her mother recounted the scene they had found when they had walked into Father Mateusz's bedroom. The doctor listened, nodding and making wordless sounds of acknowledgement as he inspected the priest's wounds. Few of the injuries to his body were serious, the doctor squeezing teat pipettes of iodine from a heavy brown bottle and dripping it over the open cuts and sores, then taking lengths of bandage fabric from Natalia, that he wrapped around the affected areas, securing them with safety pins. He worked swiftly, his fingers surprisingly agile for his age, muscle memory having built up over five decades and more.

As he peeled back the wine-red patch of blanket that they had bound to Father Mateusz's neck, he gasped. He warned the priest that he might hurt him more and moved his head a little way over to the other side. The wounds there, deep enough to expose part of the artery that throbbed with blood, gave off a sickening squelching sound as the torn sinew pulled apart and then knitted together again as he released it.

He turned to Natalia. "This is deep and quite serious. I'm afraid without antibiotics, the chance of infection means this could end up the same way as Kuba's leg." He looked over to the Natalia's mother then, his eyes seeming wary. "With your mother's permission ..." he looked back to Natalia, "... I'd like to ask you to prepare a pot of the anti-bacterial medicine that Baba Yaga made, *if* you remember what went into it?"

Natalia's mother crossed herself and mumbled something under her breath, then looked at her daughter. She nodded. "It's fine, Natka. If it's the only way." She reached out and touched Natalia's shoulder.

Natalia moved her hand, resting it on top of her mother's. She remembered every moment of the strange meeting with the witch. It was all she had been able to think about since what had happened in the woods, and this *attack* on Father Mateusz – for that's what it appeared to be – was going to bring it to mind all the more.

"I remember, Doctor. It's quite simple, in fact. Just peppermint leaves and honey. Oh and something called cinnamon bark."

"They'll have it at the bakery," her mother said. She looked down at the priest, still lying limp against her. "Father, will you allow it? The treatment?"

The priest flinched, his tongue lolling sluggishly in his mouth. Despite his pain and injuries, he managed to form the words. "If it's just a simple mixture of herbs, I see no problem with it." He started choking as he spoke, bloody saliva building in his mouth and spilling out over his torn bottom lip. Natalia's mother wiped it away with the edge of the blanket. The priest shuffled his position to look at Natalia, his skin turning pale. "Tell me Natalia, is this all the woman did? Is it this what she died for?"

Natalia felt the sorrow and regret for the old woman's death wash over her again, like a wound reopened. She scrunched her eyes shut to save herself from breaking down and looked away from the priest. She nodded sharply. Then there was silence.

CHAPTER 10

IT HAD taken persuasion verging on bullying to convince Father Mateusz to stay in Doctor Malinowski's spare room while he recovered. The doctor wanted to keep an eye on him, but with his injuries not life-threatening at this stage, the roads to the city were still too treacherous for anyone to risk transferring him to the hospital. The vicarage was still infested with thousands of creatures. Once he'd stopped protesting, Natalia and her mother had supported him on the slow walk to the doctor's house. Now they were walking, much more briskly, towards home to get cleaned up.

Natalia's mother had offered to speak to a few of the men in town after work to try to get them to come to the church and the vicarage with poison to kill the insects and rodents that were all over the place. Natalia would stay at home with Kuba, making sure he was eating, helping him to do the exercises the doctor had suggested for him to regain full use of his leg.

Her brother was in the kitchen, eating buttered toast as she walked through the door. "Where have you been?" he asked in garbled words, distorted by the fullness of his mouth. "And why are you all bloody?"

Natalia and her mother each looked at their soiled clothes, as if verifying that their bizarre morning had been real.

"First we'll get cleaned up. Then, we'll tell you. It's good to see you eating, kiddo," their mother said, gripping his shoulder and planting a kiss on his bird's nest of hair. "I'll bathe first, if it's all right with you Natka. I have to be at work in an hour."

Natalia nodded, washed her hands and sat at the table opposite her brother. She reached over and stole half a slice of his toast, stuffing a huge chunk into her mouth and biting down into it, the molten butter and crunchy crust setting one another off perfectly, all the more with an empty stomach.

"Hey! That's mine!" Kuba cried out, as if hoping their mother would hear him through the closed bathroom door. The water still flowed; it seemed he was out of luck.

"I'll make us another couple of slices in a moment. I'm *starving*. Never go on a life-or-death rescue mission before breakfast. Remember that, little brother." She took another huge bite and happily chomped it.

"A rescue mission? Who did you rescue? What happened?" Kuba lunged forward in his chair, no longer concerned with his toast.

Natalia leaned forward and beckoned to her little brother to come closer. "We had to save Father Mateusz. From what, I can't tell you until you're finished eating. It was disgusting. But I think it's to do with-"

"Baba Yaga!" The boy interrupted, his eyes alight with energy. Natalia nodded. "Natka, I have to tell you something. About a dream." He picked up his last half slice of toast and took a bite, waiting for his sister to respond.

"Tell me, little brother, then I'll slice more bread." She sat up straight, looking into the boy's eyes, assuring him he had her full attention.

He swallowed his mouthful. "Do you remember something she said in the house? The day when she mended my leg?"

"Which part?" Natalia was curious.

"The part about being the balance. I remember at the time, thinking it was a strange thing to say. Did she mean like Mum's balance, when she's making cakes in the kitchen, you know?"

Natalia chuckled at the simplicity of the boy's reasoning. "It's a bit like that, I think, Kuba. But it's a metaphor."

"Me-ta-phor?"

"It's not important. Anyway, tell me about your dream." She stood and walked to the counter and picked up the bread knife, ready to slice.

"OK, well. In the dream, there's a balance. A *huge* balance."

"A scale, like this one?" She pointed to her mother's scale on a shelf.

The boy nodded. "Exactly, but huge, *really* massive. And in one side is the village and the other side is the forest."

"Strange."

"Very strange isn't it? And then the balance – the scale – starts to burn. And the village falls down. But the forest doesn't fall down. It just grows, and the houses, the birds, everything, they grow over the houses in the village and they're all just covered. Like they're buried but under plants and animals and trees and ferns and-"

"When did you have this dream, Kuba?"

"It's been every night. Since the day she died. So it's three nights. What do you think it means?"

Natalia turned away to hide her dumbstruck facial expression. "I don't think it means anything at all. Just a dream, little brother. Now, one slice or two?" She spoke forcefully, trying to hide the stammer in her voice, then cut into the loaf.

Natalia was helping Kuba to bathe when she heard the sound. A sharp, staccato crack in the air, once, twice. Then a long period of silence before three times more, each sound echoing over the stillness of the hillside. Their mother had been at work an hour or two already.

Kuba looked up at Natalia, his expression one of puzzlement. "What was that, Natka?"

She cocked her head, listening to the quiet. "I don't know what it was, but I think it's stopped, whatever it was." She pulled the plug from the heavy, old bathtub and the water began to swirl down the plughole.

Kuba leaned on her for support as he stepped out of the bath and on to the thin bathmat where she wrapped him in a heavy towel and tousled his hair dry as he shivered in the chilly, humid air of the bathroom. Then the sound rang out again, two percussive snapping sounds. The two of them looked at each other.

"We should go and see what it is, Kuba. Let's get you dressed, all right?" She helped him into his bedroom and sat him down on the wooden chair next to his table. "I'll get some clothes for you and then give you a few minutes to get ready." Kuba nodded and waited as she pulled out the heavy drawers and took out underwear, thick socks, a long sleeved top and a jumper and placed them next to his trousers, before leaving the room.

Natalia was already in her boots and coat, holding onto Kuba's heavy winter jacket as he stepped out of his room a few minutes later. She helped him pull on the jacket and wound his scarf around his neck before leading him outside, the sound ringing again, this time just once, and much louder, now they were in the open air. It was coming from further away than the village.

Kuba realised first. "It sounds like it's coming from the farm." He was pointing as he spoke.

Natalia agreed and took his hand, leading him away from the village and towards the livestock farm further out on the outskirts. As the farm came into sight, they could see a single human form standing out near the farmhouse and several low, dark shapes moving around. The shrill cracking sound cut through the air twice more. The farmer's rifle.

Every part of Natalia told her they should move away, that this wasn't safe. But she needed to know what was happening, and all the more to know if it was connected to the woman in the forest. She turned to her brother. "Stay close to me, Kuba." The boy reached out and gripped her hand.

As they got closer, the dark shapes became clearer. They were feral dogs, two of them large enough that they might have been wolves, but it was difficult for Natalia to say. Two lay dead in the pig pen, near the bloody carcass of one of the larger pigs. Another shot went off and one of the dogs let out a high-pitched yelp as it fell onto its side. The farmer spun around to see two more dogs rounding on him, pinning him in to the wall of the farmhouse. He pulled back the bolt on his rifle and snapped in another shell. He took aim and fired, the closer of the two dogs collapsing, a fine spray of red mist dispersing behind its head.

The dog he had shot moments before was back on its feet and limping towards him. Natalia called out. "Mr. Lisowski! Behind you!"

He turned his head, following the desperate sound of her voice, a fraction of a second before the injured dog leapt up and tore at his forearm. Its jaws clamped down, teeth piercing his heavy flannel shirt and almost causing him to drop the rifle. Natalia froze. The huge man looked as though he might fall at first, before finding his balance and turning the rifle around, the wooden stock crashing into the dog's head and sending it sprawling onto the ground.

Lisowski rotated the rifle again and took aim at the dazed dog as it struggled to find its feet. This time, he made no mistake, bullets puncturing its forehead and chest, the body left quivering at his feet. Only two dogs were left standing now, too far apart to effectively operate as a pack. One backed away, its eyes focussed on the farmer as it retreated. The second looked up and made eye contact with Natalia, before bowing its head again and darting straight past them towards the village without looking back, Natalia holding her brother close to protect him.

The farmer swung his rifle over his shoulder with its leather strap and walked toward Natalia and her brother, clutching his bloodied elbow and forearm.

"Natalia, are you both all right?" he said as he got close to them. "What are you kids doing up here?" He unravelled the rope which closed the gate and swung the big wooden structure open, beckoning them onto his land, his eyes wide with concern.

"Sorry, Mr. Lisowski, we just heard noises." Natalia nodded towards the gun on his back. "We wanted to see what was happening. Things have been... strange... since the other day in the woods."

"I don't even want to hear about it, truth be told. I was asked to come to your blessing and to that... whatever it ended up being at the old house. I stayed away. I wanted no part of it. I knew it would get out of hand. That bishop is far more adept at whipping up a crowd than following the teachings of his religion. But it was wrong what they did out there."

Kuba stepped away from his sister and spoke up first. "Baba Yaga was kind to me. She didn't use any *magic*. The bishop was a *liar*."

Natalia pulled him back to her, trying to hush him. "Do you need help with that arm?" Natalia knew Mrs. Lisowska was working with her mother, at the embroidery house. The farmer rubbed the wound through his shirt, shaking his head.

"I reckon it'll be not much more than a flesh wound. I'll be all right."

Natalia nodded and went to turn back towards home and then stopped herself. She looked at the farmer. "Why did you say it was wrong, Mr.

Lisowski? What happened to Baba Yaga, I mean."

There was a long silence, the farmer looking up the field to the slaughtered pig, steam rising from its body and those of its canine assailants that lay beside it in death. He looked back to her.

"Can I offer you both some tea? It's still cold out." He turned and walked back up to the house without waiting for a reply.

Natalia looked at Kuba, the boy already tugging at her to follow the farmer. She smiled at her brother and they walked together across the field and into the farmhouse.

The two children sat on one of the long benches beside the huge dark wood table in the farmer's kitchen. Lisowski walked over to the fire and used a towel to take a dark iron kettle from over the flames, filling three cups with an amber coloured liquid. He replaced the kettle and unscrewed the cap from a clear, unlabelled bottle, pouring a few drops of a clear liquid into his and Natalia's cups. After setting the cups down he walked into a large larder, returning with a rolled poppy seed cake and two small plates. He severed off two generous slices and positioned them in front of Natalia and her brother.

"Left over from the new year. She makes good poppy seed roulade, Mrs. Lisowksa."

Natalia made to express her gratitude but was put off by the sight of her brother already stuffing a huge chunk into his face in her peripheral vision. She let out a simple thank you and took a bite.

They ate quietly, each of them pretending not to watch too closely as the farmer rolled up his sleeve and cleaned the bite marks over the low metal basin. Once it was clean, he returned to the table and sat opposite them, holding a fresh towel to his injuries to stem the blood flow.

Natalia put what was left of her cake down and asked again. "Why did you think it was wrong, Mr. Lisowski?"

He took a sip of his tea and then looked above the children's heads, his eyes hazing over. "What did you talk to her about, when you went out there to the forest? Both of you?"

Natalia shrugged and recounted what she could recall about the conversation with Baba Yaga. About how she'd asked her about the rumours of Satanism and her statements about balance. Kuba joined in at this point, referencing his strange dreams, until Natalia hushed him again.

The farmer nodded and listened as she explained, periodically sipping at his vodka-infused tea and then wiping his beard with his good forearm. When she reached the end, he took out an old clay pipe and began to thumb clumps of tobacco down into it. "Did she tell you her name?" The words were almost an afterthought, something that just occurred to him as he was preparing to smoke.

"It was Julia," said Kuba, very matter-of-factly.

The farmer stood and left the kitchen, the big

man's footsteps audible and present as he walked through the house and up the stairs. Natalia and Kuba looked at one another, unsure what was happening. After a few moments, Lisowski stomped back into the kitchen, setting down a battered old journal on the table. He thumbed through the pages until an old, faded black-and-white photograph fell out of the pages. He shoved it across the table towards Natalia.

There was Lisowski Senior, the farmer's father, who Natalia remembered from her early childhood. He'd been dead a decade or more already. Beside him was his wife, still living upstairs in the house they were in today, though bedridden for much of the time – she had to be at least ninety years old. They were holding a baby.

"Is that you?" Natalia pointed to the child. The farmer nodded.

"But it's not about me, it's about her." He leaned over the table and placed his huge forefinger above a younger woman on the other side of his father. Natalia looked closely at her. There was a definite resemblance to the older Mr. Lisowski, but what was now clear was that she was the old woman from the forest.

"Julia." She covered her mouth after she said it, then looked up at the farmer.

He smiled, thick crows' feet wrinkling beside his eyes as he did so. "She told me, when I was a toddler – three years old or something, you know?

She told me about the balance. Everything she told you both when you were out there." He drained what was left of his tea. "She told me the Baba Yaga was dying. That, when she did, the balance would disappear. That nature would overcome us – more so here in this wild part of the world than perhaps anywhere. And then she disappeared."

"She went to become the new Baba Yaga?"

"My dad knew. He knew but he didn't tell me until right before he died. He promised her he wouldn't tell anyone, not even me. So I never went out there. Never saw her. And now… well…"

"And now everything she said would happen is happening. The balance is broken, skewed. And nature is taking control."

The farmer closed his eyes. "I've been working this land – at first with my father of course – for nigh on fifty years and I've never had feral dogs attack my livestock like that. The pig, a couple sheep, all the chickens – about thirty head of livestock dead today. And they were coordinated. The feral dogs from the woods, working together. That doesn't happen."

"Oh, that isn't the half of it," said Natalia. She went on to explain the incident at the church and the state she'd found the house in the woods in after the burning, both her brother and the farmer wide-eyed as they each learned about those events for the first time. When she finished explaining everything she knew they all sat quietly at the table for a moment.

"Where does it all end?" the farmer asked aloud. He paused before answering his own question. "That's something none of us knows. But I suppose we're going to find out."

CHAPTER 11

NATALIA stood alone, in a darkness the likes of which she could never have even imagined, let alone seen before. It was like a heavy liquid, seeping into everything and weighing her down, inside and out. She spun around, looking for she-didn't-know-what, and finding nothing but more impenetrable blackness. She stepped backwards and walked into something solid. She turned around, but, even at such close quarters, could see nothing. She reached out with her hands and felt the uneven grain of wood. Not a tree, but cut wood. A structure.

She ran her hands up it, feeling for a feature or a groove that might indicate to her what it was, then suddenly it was illuminated by a source she couldn't locate. A tower of rough-hewn wood reached high up in to the sky. It was narrow – just wider than she was herself – and it went straight up as far as she could see. She stepped backwards, and the illumination spread outward, revealing a colossal wooden scale with rusted iron chains suspending plates on either side. On the first plate was the forest, dark, creatures moving in shadow one way and the other. On the second was the village in microcosm. The church and her home were represented at the very centre.

The scale tipped one way and the other, the scales finding balance. They stopped in the middle, swaying. Natalia felt a sense of peace, of calm. Then she saw a flickering beneath her feet. Tongues of flame, at first just a few centimetres tall, licked at the grasses covering the ground and bloomed out from beneath her until the ground was a carpet of dancing fire.

Smoke began to emerge from the base of the scale before a bright burst of green sparks spewed forth from it and it was transformed – an emerald pyre, engulfed in its entirety. Natalia unconsciously took another step back, but she couldn't stop looking, couldn't flee. There was nowhere to go. Nowhere but the dark.

She watched as the fire ate at the beam of the scale, the wood diminishing as the blaze devoured it. The plates began to swing, gently at first, then more violently until the whole structure shuddered, a deafening, splintering crack occupying the darkness in its entirety. The beam tilted toward the village, the plate it sat upon almost touching the ground. Then the forest was tumbling, as if in slow motion, the plants and trees writhing, shadows blurring one way and the other until it was on top of the village. The tendrils of vines wrapped around the tower of the church and then spread out across the other buildings, while shadowy forms crashed through windows and doors, until all was overrun. A singular wilderness. The sole remaining sign of human life was the screaming, a dozen voices and more wailing in unison.

And then she was awake.

Her sweat-soaked chest heaved as she found herself sitting up in the more familiar darkness of her bedroom.

Then she felt them. The eyes.

She looked around, but could find nothing. Still she felt the gaze on her, penetrating deep into her. She lay back down and pulled the blankets up over her head. Her pulse was a heavy, blasting drumbeat in her ears now, her breath quick and shallow.

"The balance is lost," said a deep voice, neither masculine nor feminine, from somewhere in the room.

Natalia peeled the blanket away and peered through the murk at her mother, who sat bolt upright, her eyes wide open.

"Lost, and with it the hope of your kind," her mother said, in a voice not her own.

"Mum?"

There was no reply. Only silence.

"Oh my God." Natalia jumped from the bed and

knelt, beginning to mouth a silent prayer.

"I am so much *older* than your god, girl. It holds no sway over me nor my dominion."

Natalia lowered her hands, mid-action, and turned to face her mother directly. Her mother's eyes were rolled back, the whites almost filling the sockets, yet somehow she could still feel her mother − or whatever was controlling her − staring at her. Sizing her up.

"What do you want from me? From us?" Natalia fired the question with more venom than she had intended, and feared she may have enraged it.

It sat, hands rubbing together in its lap, staring at her without blinking. "The balance is lost and what I want is of no consequence to you. What I offer might be."

Natalia moved up to sit on the edge of her bed, to be on eye level with it. She wondered if this was not an extension of her dream. "What you offer? I don't understand?"

"I am the spirit of the forest, of the desert plains, of the Arctic tundra and of the deepest trenches of the ocean. The god of what your filthy kind has yet to touch and infect. There are times I would have it that nature were allowed to develop freely, to strangle you and your miserable species from existence." The thing reached out toward Natalia with its hands, making a choking action.

Natalia sat, silent. She felt powerless, alone in this room with whatever it was that had hold of her mother. She took a deep breath and summoned the courage to speak. "And yet you would offer me... my kind... something? What is it? And why, if we are so loathsome?"

Her mother's body lurched forward, casting the blankets from her legs and onto the floor. She paced across the room, stopping with barely a hair's breadth between her and Natalia. "Your species is unique. No other mortal being possesses a consciousness. It would be a shame to see that spark turn to an ember – to ash – because of your frailty. So I seek out those who understand. Who understand what it means to truly maintain the balance. To hold the appetites of man at bay with one hand and to unite them with the natural world with the other."

"Baba Yaga," Natalia said the words as much to herself as to the thing.

"Your 'Baba Yaga' is just the name your people give it. Such figures are everywhere. Maintaining the balance. And you, Natalia, can be one such person. But this role is one of sacrifice, this you must understand well before we can proceed."

Natalia ran her hands through her hair, tying it off in a bun behind her head. She rubbed her eyes and then closed them tight. She looked at her mother again. "If I were to accept your offer, if I were to become the next Baba Yaga or *balance* – whatever you want to call it – what is *my* sacrifice? What is at stake?"

The thing in her mother smiled and sat back on the edge of her bed. She clasped her hands together, as if excited by the prospect of closing the deal. "The first sacrifice is a life of solitude. To be at one with nature is to live amongst it, to feel it, to *taste* it. You will give up these tools of man." It gestured to the electric lamp next to her bed. "Your light will be from candles, your food from the wilds, heat from the fire and entertainment from the kinship you will share with the forces with which you co-exist."

Natalia nodded, unperturbed by such things. It didn't seem so bad lined up against a future limited to marriage, producing as many children as her future husband desired and then tending the home with an outside chance of a job doing embroidery or another 'woman's job.'

"I am not yet finished," it went on. "You are an intelligent young woman. You will have noticed the attacks of the natural world have targeted specific victims, no?"

Natalia had obviously noticed. "Those involved with Baba Yaga's execution."

The thing nodded in response. "Precisely, the cruel end of the balance." The thing stood and paced the length of the room, then back. It looked at Natalia again with those bulging white eyes. "Who remains? From your village folk, who is yet to be punished for this by the savage lands?"

Natalia brought her hand up to her chin. "The

pub owner, Piotr. He was the one who started the fire, spread the fuel."

"And stopped the attack on that self-righteous churchman from the city," the thing said, scarcely attempting to conceal its disgust.

"So I must watch as he is struck down in vengeance before I can restore balance? Is this your concept of justice?"

The thing stood, raising its hand to strike. "The burning of the balance was yours!" Its shriek permeated Natalia's skull with its pitch and ferocity.

"Very well. Then I will agree to it. I will become the new balance. I will be your new Baba Yaga." She stood and reached out her hand to close the deal, but the thing swiped it away.

"I am yet to finish, child. Sit."

Natalia sat.

Waited.

"There is another whose role was crucial in the fall of the balance. Another who is yet to experience due retribution for their crime."

Natalia closed her eyes and bit her bottom lip, to ward off the emotions boiling inside and threatening to overcome her. She started shaking her head. "No. I won't. I can't. I simply cannot."

"It was she who instigated the persecution. She too must be ended, before balance can be restored."

Natalia felt a single tear escape her twitching left eye and roll, cold, down her hot cheek. "My mother. You want me to watch my mother die by your hand before I commune with you and become the new bond between your world and my own. Do you understand what you are asking?"

"This decision is not mine to make! This body ..." The thing tugged at the skin around the collar bone, the forearm, the cheek. "This body will be drained of life, whether you sit at the division between the wild and your kind or not. The question is not 'will you watch your mother die?' but rather, 'will you watch her *alone* die, or will you and everyone you know be interred with her?'" The thing sat back, leaning on its hands, smiling.

"I need some time to decide. This is too much for me at this moment." Natalia wiped a trail of mucus from under her nose, her tears now flowing freely.

"I understand. You have one week." And the voice was gone. Her mother fell back, her body a limp bag of meat and bones, eyes closed on the bed. Natalia dashed across the gap between the two beds and dropped to her knees.

Her mother was was still breathing. Natalia leaned forward, lifting her left eyelid. Normal. She covered her with her blankets and got back into bed. She pulled the cover up to her neck and closed her eyes.

She thought she could hear something moving outside the door but, before she could react, sleep crept up on her, dragging her off into a dreamless nothingness.

CHAPTER 12

SHE SAT bolt upright, hours later when she woke up. Light was streaming in through the curtains at the other side of the bedroom. She looked over at her mother's bunk. Empty. She climbed out of bed, stuffing her feet into her warm slippers, and opened the bedroom door. Her mother was in the kitchen, vigorously beating a thick-looking mixture in a large ceramic bowl.

"Morning, Natka. I'm making potato pancakes for breakfast, are you hungry?"

Natalia had to think about the question for far longer than usual before nodding. She sat down at the table and poured herself a cup of tea from the pot, wisps of steaming vapour rising from the hot liquid.

Within a few minutes, she and her mother sat in front of plates of crispy, fried potato pancakes, dropping crumbly slices of white cheese on top and quietly eating. After a few minutes, Natalia spoke. "Are you feeling all right today, Mum?"

Her mother put down her knife and fork with a chinking sound and looked at her. She wiped her mouth with a napkin. "I feel fine. A bit tired. Why do you ask?"

Natalia shovelled another piece of pancake into her mouth and chewed it, smiling at the crisp texture of the outer edge, in contrast with the soft, doughy middle. She swallowed. "You were talking in your sleep, that's all. You don't remember?"

Her mother shook her head. "How strange. I don't know that I've ever done it before. It must be all my worrying about Kuba."

This sparked Natalia's mind into action. "Where is Kuba?" She looked across at the wall clock – already ten in the morning.

"The doctor said he needs rest, Natka. For the time being, I'm letting him sleep as long as he wants." Her mother picked up her cutlery again and started on her second pancake, occasionally pausing for a sip of tea. "What do you have lined up for today?"

Natalia scooped the last forkful of food into her mouth and then drained the dregs of her tea. "I was thinking about taking a walk. The sun's out. The cold isn't as bad as it has been. You can join me if you like?"

Her mother stood up, carrying the dishes over to the large metal sink and began running the water. "I would do. But today I wanted to get some seeds in the ground and to be here for Kuba. You don't mind going alone, no?"

"Not at all. Thanks for breakfast, Mum. I'm going to go and have a wash and get dressed." Natalia waved and dashed back to the bedroom.

It would have been a good way to tarnish her reputation, standing outside the pub with the spring sun still not at its highest point. The place didn't even open until noon, but here she was, not long after eleven. Waiting.

Piotr, the pub owner – no-one had used his family name, Niemiecki, "the German" since the war – slept upstairs in a bedsit of sorts which had been there when he bought the place. Natalia had never been up there, naturally, but the rumour was that it was basic at best, and the low ceilings were something of a challenge for the great bear of a man Piotr was. She glanced up to the single window and noted that the curtains were drawn, no lights on, despite the pub being shaded by the church tower at this hour. He must still have been asleep.

But Natalia knew he was next. The spirit of the wilderness had told her as much. She had to wake him up. She went to the door and found there was no knocker. Indeed, why would there be when the pub was open from noon until the early hours every day? She looked around for something hard but not too heavy and found a few pebbly chunks of rock beyond the path. She scampered over and picked up a handful, before returning and tossing them, one-by-one at the closed window. She missed with the first couple of shots but, once she had her eye in, she hit the target once, twice. She lined up a third and was winding up to throw it when the curtain stirred and the hulking, neckless form of Piotr appeared.

He released a loud yawn as he pushed the window wide open on its hinge and then said, "We're not open for another hour. And you're too young to be served alcohol anyway. Go away!" He slammed the window shut and aggressively pulled the curtains closed.

Natalia looked around. The village was quiet. The door to the post office was open but, other than that, there were no obvious signs of life. No signs of *threat*. She released the breath which she hadn't even realised she'd been holding. He was safe. For now, at least.

She walked across the square and sat on the bench outside the church, training her eyes on the pub. There was no movement. She wished she had brought her book along, but then she hadn't anticipated Piotr being so resistant to being woken up. She was going over what to say to him for the tenth time when she noticed something stirring in one of the downstairs windows. Curtains being drawn back. Natalia stood up and walked to the entrance, just catching the sound of the locks being opened on the front door as she got closer.

The door swung inwards and she stepped forward into the doorway. "Piotr," she said with real enthusiasm.

The huge man tipped backwards on his heels, his expression one of shock. "Natalia. What are you doing here? I told you I'll not serve you, so why don't you just clear off?" He shoved the door forward, Natalia holding up her right hand, blocking it and feeling pain in her wrist from the force of it.

"Your life is in mortal danger and if you don't listen to me now, you may not see the sunset tonight." Natalia's words were cold, matter-of-fact, bereft of any emotion. The huge man frowned, as if expecting her to burst into laughter after her little joke. She stood perfectly still, her expression blank.

"All right, all right, come in and tell me what the hell you're talking about." He made space for her to pass him and then motioned for her to sit at one of the cushioned benches, near the high tables. He followed and sat opposite, the bulk of him always surprising at close quarters. "I'm ready," Piotr said, more than a hint of agitation in his voice.

Natalia looked at her hands, folded neatly together on the table in front of her. She began with the jackdaw's attack on the bishop after the execution and went through the near-death of Father Mateusz, the wild dogs' run on the livestock farm of Mr Lisowski, and she recounted the dream and her mother's channelling of the spirit.

Piotr was a simple man and a God-fearing one. It was why he'd been so eager to take so full a part in the burning of the *witch*. He was pale by the end of Natalia's explanation, his gargantuan shape somehow diminished. He heaved himself up from the table and paced to the bar and back. He went to speak and paused, then began pacing once more. He didn't seem to know what to do. He took down a bottle of vodka from the top shelf of his bar collection and came back to the table. He filled a shot glass and motioned towards Natalia, offering her some. She waved away the drink. He picked up the glass and looked at Natalia.

"To our health," he said and swallowed the liquor straight down. He placed the glass back down on the table and returned the bottle to the bar area. Then he sat in front of Natalia again. "So it's true what they've been saying? The church is ruined?"

Natalia thought she detected despair in his voice. She reached forward and placed a hand on his forearm, which she noticed was trembling.

"It's not *ruined*. But Father Mateusz has to request the extermination of the insects and rodents. He'd hoped a few of the village men could handle it, but it's too severe. They need poison, traps, and so on. It's going to be off limits for a few weeks, at least."

He looked into her eyes. "But how am I to save myself if I can't even be with God? Can't ask for forgiveness?" Within the huge shell of the man, Natalia saw the frightened little boy that Piotr was. His parents both dead. An only child. Never married. Alone in the world.

"Don't say that, Piotr. God will still hear your prayers, whether you're in the church or right here in the pub. But the threat to your life is real. When is your next delivery?"

He looked over his shoulder, his eyes running over the barrels and bottles on the shelves. He turned back to her. "A week or so. We're well stocked and people come out less at this time of year."

Natalia nodded, a new well of confidence that she might be able to save his life welling inside of her. "And how about supplies for you? Do you have enough food to lie low for a few days?"

Piotr took back his log of an arm and scratched his wrist with the other hand. "I've got a full larder and cold store. Lisowski even sold me a couple rabbits he'd shot. They're hanging up outside, so I think I'll manage."

Natalia smiled at him. "I want you to stay here, Piotr, just for a few days. Until we can figure out how to stop this *force*, whatever it is, from harming you. Is that all right?"

Piotr sat forward, leaning on the table with all his weight. "Can I still open and have customers in?"

Natalia stood up and began putting on her coat. "I think that will be fine. But keep your rifle behind the counter, just in case, eh?"" She finished dressing for the cold and then went to the door, pulling the heavy iron handle and stepping out. As the door was closing, Piotr called out to her.

"Natalia! Thank you for warning me. And sorry. For being so angry when you woke me up."

"Don't worry about it. I'll see you in a few days." She waved and let the door swing closed, before heading off into the chilly headwind towards home.

CHAPTER 13

TWO DAYS passed without event. Kuba continued with his recovery, though still subdued, compared to before the accident. Their mother had put that down to the end of the winter break and the prospect of school restarting over in the next village in a week or so. There had been no further attacks by the spirit of the wilderness, so, while she kept her eye firmly on her mother for any signs of trouble, Natalia felt confident that, for now at least, things were more or less normal.

The sun was shining and the corner of their house acted as a perfect windbreak, so Natalia was outside on a wooden chair she'd brought from the kitchen, enjoying the feeling of warm sunshine on her face and reading. She didn't even notice Lisowski coming up the path from the village, his breath short, until he spoke.

"Natalia, you need to come quick. It's

happened."

She closed her book and looked up, startled. "I don't understand, what's happened?"

"Piotr."

"I told him to stay at home. What the hell?"

"He *stayed* at home. But... I don't know how to explain. It's better if you just come."

Natalia stood up and tightened her scarf around her neck. She fastened the top two buttons on her heavy jacket and followed as Lisowski led the way, several paces ahead. When they arrived at the town square it was immediately obvious why he hadn't been able to explain.

The walls, door and windows of the pub were a criss-cross of vines and creepers. Flowers bloomed on delicate stems which spewed forth from the intricate web of plant material.

Natalia turned to Lisowski. "Is it like this all over?" The farmer nodded. Natalia let out a pained sigh. She stepped forward and grabbed a handful of plant material and started to tug at it, releasing it as the bramble thorns shredded her skin. "Ouch!" She looked back to Lisowski. "Do you have any gloves?"

The farmer held up some working gloves, then tossed a pair over to Natalia. She plucked them from the air as they sailed towards her, momentarily looking at the fine trails of blood which decorated her palm before putting them on. Then they got to work, pulling and heaving at the woven plant matter that covered the building. It was difficult, exhausting work. Single strands of plant were half a dozen metres long or more, making finding a point to attack and to rip nearly impossible. The capacity of the ivy-like creepers to hold on against human strength was remarkable. Lisowski worked with a pocket knife, severing the long strands, while Natalia followed up, tugging the tangled remains away from the surface. After 30 minutes or more, they had revealed the majority of the door.

Lisowski dropped his knife at his feet and beat at the door with all his strength. The building shook with the force of it. "Piotr, are you in there? Say something if you can hear me!"

Silence.

He looked over at Natalia, who was leaning against the wall, catching her breath. "We're going to have to force the door, once we've cleared this off."

Natalia frowned. "Do you know how heavy this door is?"

Lisowski managed a smile at the question. "I've drunk here two nights a week for nearly thirty years. I know it well. But there's no other way in. The back door is covered with a metal grate."

Natalia let out another frustrated sigh and nodded her acceptance. She turned back around and started pulling at the loose plant material again while Lisowski reached down for his knife. They set to work for another hour before the door was completely uncovered. Lisowski cast his knife to the ground and helped Natalia with the last few stubborn tendrils of plant matter, wrenching them from the wall and throwing them onto a pile on the ground.

He motioned for Natalia to stand back, then aimed his foot at the locking mechanism of the arched wooden door. He took several steps backward and then strode forward, following through with his boot. His kick smashed the panel of wood at the lock, sawdust and splinters flying up into the air. He found his balance and then shoved the door in completely, Natalia doing her best to help.

Inside they were greeted with an earthy smell, the fragrance of damp soil, of plants breathing. The walls and ceiling were completely coated in thick moss, while the floor and tables were overrun with more of the thin brambles and creepers. Bright yellow fungus grew at odd angles from the stems of tables and chair legs. It seemed like the place had been abandoned for years. Natalia was taken back to Baba Yaga's house, two days after the execution. She recalled the stillness, the sense of the wilderness having reclaimed the stone cottage and the eyes – not to mention the breath – of the lynx on her.

She was stirred from her reverie by Lisowski's voice. "The stairs are through the back. Come on." She nodded and followed the farmer through the door at the rear of the bar area. They walked through the kitchen, the metallic surfaces rusted while the floor and walls were similarly overgrown with weeds and moss. They walked through the swing doors at the back and out to the stairs.

Lisowski stepped up first, his foot slipping on the slick surface of densely packed moss. He almost fell, but managed to right himself. He turned back to Natalia. "Hold the rail tight. This stuff is miserably slippery." Natalia reached out a hand and clutched the rail with all the strength she had left. They carefully ascended, their feet never quite finding their grip. At the top of the stairs the farmer nodded towards the door in front. "That's the bathroom. Piotr's bedroom is at the other end of the landing."

Natalia looked over at the door, left ajar. She followed Lisowski along the short landing until he stopped outside. A rank smell seeped from the room.

"This might not be pleasant," he said. "If you want to wait outside while I check-"

"No. I made it my duty to protect Piotr after I spoke to the wilderness spirit. I thought I was doing that by telling him to stay here. If he has perished because of it, I want to face it." Natalia's expression was hard, determined. Lisowski said nothing more and pushed open the door.

The waft of decay became an all-consuming wave, the scent driving Natalia to the edge of vomiting. She raised one hand and covered her mouth and nose. Piotr's colossal frame was entombed in weeds, thin stems knitted together into a soft, green sarcophagus. There was no sign of breathing, his barrel chest unmoving. Everything in the room was still. His head and shoulders, at the top of the bed were still in shadow. With Lisowski motionless at the door, crossing himself, Natalia stepped further into the room and gasped.

The green death cloak stopped above the shoulders, revealing the pale skin at the throat. His mouth hung open, brambles like stitches woven in and out of the now blue lips. Where his eyes once were, two poppies had bloomed, their dense black stamens coated with seeds at the centre of the paper-like red petals. Natalia felt a shiver run down her spine, her perception skewed, as though she had shifted, far from the scene. She stared at the huge shape of Piotr, someone she had sworn to protect, now laying still, gone ... his body no more than a fertile host for the plants which encased him.

"It doesn't look like he suffered," said Liswoski, coming closer. Natalia felt herself present in the moment once more. The farmer was right. "This is exactly how she described it to me, you know?" He was leaning against the far wall, unable to take his eyes from Piotr's body.

Natalia looked up. "Who do you mean?"

"My aunt Julia. When she told my father of her plans, it was after she'd been to see Baba Yaga. She'd been found her dead in the house, the whole place overgrown. And the body..." he trailed off and made a gesture towards Piotr, lying still on the bed.

Natalia took in a sharp breath. "It was the same last week. Your aunt... I mean, I didn't see the body but, all this. This plant life, the moss, the woven creepers covering the door. It was all the same."

Lisowski held a hand up to his mouth, a single tear tracing a path down his cheek before dripping down onto his jacket. "She's as one with nature in death, as in life. Good." He cleared his throat and then smiled through the pain he was clearly feeling. "There's nothing we can do here. Let's get home, eh?" He put his hand on Natalia's shoulder and she moved closer, the warmth of a hug exactly what she needed.

"Sorry, Piotr," she whispered, as they left the room.

CHAPTER 14

FOR THE following three days, Natalia was her mother's shadow. After telling Piotr of his fate and the devastating results that had ensued, she'd decided it was better for her mother not to know of the time bomb ticking above her head. Instead, she claimed she needed air when her mother set off for work and volunteered to go in her place when errands needed running outside the house. With Kuba still spending much of his time with his leg elevated, she would rarely be at home alone.

It was sometime after lunch on the third day that her mother declared she needed to go to post a letter to her sister, who lived far across the country, in Katowice. Natalia was exhausted, but she couldn't risk her mother going alone with this death warrant hanging over her. She stood up from her chair, closing her book and reaching across the table with an open hand. "Give it to me and I'll take it."

Her mother rolled her eyes. "Can I not leave this house for any purpose but to go to work, Natalia?" Natalia shrugged her shoulders.

"Fine, I guess you can go, but I'll come too. I need to-"

"Get some air? A bit of exercise? What is wrong with you, lately, girl?"

"Nothing's wrong. I'm just glad the winter is over and I can enjoy the outdoors more."

"What happened to my daughter who was always most contented curled up her bed with a book?"

Natalia's eyes lowered towards the book she'd just closed, the rose back to meet her mother's. "I still love books, Mum, but I need to get outside. So, shall we?" She paced back to the bedroom and tossed the book onto her bed, then grabbed her coat and scarf from the rack beside the front door.

Her mother crossed the kitchen, opened a drawer and pulled out the white envelope which contained her letter. She checked the address was complete and then put her coat on. "We're off to the post office, Kuba, all right?"

The boy looked up from the kitchen table where he was drawing with crayons, a scene that resembled the village square, indiscernible black flecks cutting through the air like elongated rain drops. The handful of buildings were vibrant and colourful, apart from the church which was brown and grey, subdued. He nodded. "See you later,

Mum. Love you." He grinned and went back to his drawing.

"That picture looks a bit sinister, brother," Natalia said, twisting her neck to get a better view of it. "Why is the rain so weird?"

The boy shrugged his shoulders. "It was a dream. It wasn't exactly like this, but I can't fully remember. Anyway, see you later." He lowered his head, grasped his blue crayon and continued filling in the sky.

Natalia and her mother strolled to the post office, enjoying the warmth of the spring sunshine and a wind whose bite had melted away with the snow. When they arrived, the post office was deserted. The postmaster's wife manned the desk, presiding over the empty space. She smiled as they entered, and Natalia decided to take a look around while her mother paid for the postage and sent the letter. There were photographs on the wall, detailing the rebuilding of the village and of the two nearest cities after the war. Natalia hadn't been in to see the images in some time, so she took a moment to pore over them.

While she was looking, the door swung open and Father Mateusz walked in, still wearing bandages on parts of his face and around his neck. Their eyes met and she walked over to greet him.

"How are you feeling, Father?" she asked quietly,

not wanting to draw unwanted attention to him.

"Thanks to you both," he said, nodding towards her mother at the counter, "I'm doing all right. My legs are still torn up and I don't know how long I'll be stuck with Malinowski reminding me about my fruit and vegetable intake... but I'm well. Recovering, let's say." He smiled.

"That's good." She returned his smile.

"I understand it was you and old Lisowski that found Piotr the other day? I was so sorry to hear about it."

Natalia nodded. "It was the same... force, I want to call it... which attacked you, Father. I was warned in a dream."

The priest's face was grave as he heard her words. "Is that so? Was there anything else this *force* told you?"

Natalia inhaled deeply and looked down at her shoes.

The priest reached out with one hand and squeezed her shoulder comfortingly. "If you'd rather talk about this somewhere private..."

"No. No, it's fine. I can tell you here." She breathed out a long sigh, shaking her head. "It said nature would sweep the entire village. We'd be extinguished, unless I became the next balance – the next Baba Yaga."

The priest took in a sharp breath. "And? Do you mean to do so?"

Natalia shook her head, her words hushed to a

whimper. "It said my mum will have to die even if I do, so what's the point?" Then she fell silent as the sound of her mother's footsteps approached.

"Father, how are you?" her mother asked, a genuine smile blooming on her face at seeing him up and about after the ordeal.

Natalia zoned out as they chatted, her thoughts trailing off, until she heard her name, not much more than a whisper. She looked around and saw the postmaster's wife beckoning her over. She hardly knew the woman, but paced over to see what she wanted.

"My dear," the woman said. "It must have been so painful to have found Piotr in such a state." She extended her hand and Natalia reached out to take it. The woman's eyes immediately rolled back as her hand clung to Natalia's. The deep voice that had been ever-present in her mind for the last five days began to speak. "The time has come for your decision, Natalia. The people will gather in the square this very afternoon. The question is how many will perish. The answer lies with you alone."

Natalia shivered, the fear-borne taste of metal in her mouth. "But it's not today. You said a week. It's the fifth day. I'm not ready."

"I said a week, but there is one remaining soul which needs to pay. I'm sure we both want this to be over, one way or another."

"Natka, let's go!" Her mother called from over by the door, as Father Mateusz left.

"Just a minute, Mum," Natalia tried and failed to conceal her anguish. She looked back to the old woman, whose face betrayed no signs of emotion, her eyes still a milky, vein-scored white.

"When the bells chime." The woman shivered, her eyes returning to normal. "It must have been just awful for you, you poor thing."

Natalia felt an uncomfortable dryness in her mouth. She nodded in agreement. "Yes, it was. I feel so bad for what happened to him. We all do, I suppose. Anyway, I must be off." She took her hand from her pocket to wave and then saw how violently it was trembling and thought better of it.

"See you," said the postmaster's wife, seemingly oblivious to everything that had just happened, a warm smile turning up her pursed lips.

CHAPTER 15

NATALIA was eating a bowl of cabbage and mushroom dumplings, topped with fried bacon and oil, as she read. She glanced over at the clock. Almost four. Her mother was outside, inserting thin pieces of guide wood and tying off runner bean plants, to ensure they grew straight. The door was open, a fresh, spring-scented breeze creeping into the house which was pleasant, even if a little cold. Natalia scooped the last chunk of dumpling into her mother and then wiped her lips on a napkin, before rinsing the bowl in the sink. She began to pour herself a cup of tea but almost dropped the teapot at a sudden sound.

The church bells.

When the bells chime.

Her mother turned around from what she was doing, looking at Natalia through the crack in the door. "Do you think they've killed all the vermin in the church already?"

Natalia felt her skin rise into goosebumps. She shrugged her shoulders. "It didn't look that way this morning, did it?"

"You're right. And Father Mateusz is still staying with the doctor. We should go and see what's going on." She laid down the length of wood she was holding in the vegetable bed and rubbed her hands together, the excess soil falling to the ground in moist clumps.

Natalia brought her hands up to her face. She felt powerless. She knew this was it, the moment she'd been warned about, but the whole thing was on rails. Impossible to affect the outcome. Finally she had a thought and revealed her face again. "What about Kuba? Shouldn't we stay here and watch him? His leg's still not right."

"Oh, he's off playing with young Aleks, the butcher's boy. He'll be fine. I'll get my coat." She brushed past Natalia and into the kitchen. She washed her hands at the sink and then dried them off on a ragged looking towel hanging next to the cooker. She then paced to the front door where she turned around sharply. "Are you just going to stay here, Natka?"

Natalia took a single sip of her tea and threw the rest into the sink. She locked the back door and walked over to her mother, who handed her her coat. She put it on and they set off for the square.

Gusts of wind blew almost rhythmically across the plains, heaving the bells and causing them to ring out, a discordant music of sorts. The village folk were almost all present. The postmaster and his wife, the butcher; Lisowski had come down from his farm. The old man who ran the general store stood outside, using his hand to block out the dazzling spring sunshine as he peered up at the church bells. The people looked at one another. With the sky so clear, such wind was unnatural, strange, and no one had ever heard the bells ring out from the force of the wind alone.

Natalia and her mother stood in the centre of the square, taking the scene in, Natalia feeling the dull thud of her heart accelerate and grow in intensity, pounding in her chest. Lisowski raised a hand in greeting when he saw them, his face pale, and carrying a tense expression that well reflected the maelstrom of fear and apprehension Natalia was feeling herself.

Some time later, Father Mateusz arrived, the doctor just behind him. Natalia's mother saw him first and called out, over the peal of the bells. "Do you know what's happening, Father?"

The priest looked at her and went to speak, his mouth opening and closing several times, without him being able to find the words he wanted. Finally, he managed, "There's no one in there, Beata. It can't be anything but this wind."

A great howling gale swept across the village square as he said it, bringing with it a great flock of birds. There were a variety of corvids in the black shape, which melted across the sky as a single, amorphous mass, twisting and turning as the birds turned this way and that. The raucous sound of their cawing was deafening, individual sounds lost in the wall of noise. They swooped around the church tower, the bells still swinging back and forth in the wind, and then turned to fly directly up, beyond the tarnished, metallic cross that adorned the building and almost out of sight. The sound of their caws reduced to a murmur.

Natalia's mother shook her arm. "What the hell is going on?" she said, her voice trembling. Natalia held on to her mother's hand and pointed up into the sky.

"They're coming back! Get down," she said, then she cried out to the people gathered there in the square. "Everyone! Get down!"

Everyone heard her, such was the force of her scream but, such is the nature of human kind, only her mother and Lisowski heeded her advice and threw themselves to the ground, hands held over their heads. The other villagers turned, first to look at Natalia and then to see what she was screaming about. By then it was too late.

The butcher, the tallest of those gathered, was the first to be struck, a great raven darting into him with immense force, its wings wide open and beating rhythmically as it used its claws and beak to strike at his face, neck and hands as he struggled on the floor. Father Mateusz, too, once more found himself under attack, two smaller crows pecking at his bandaged neck and face and drawing blood, beginning to pull stringy strands of flesh from the exposed wounds. Natalia watched all of this through the gaps in her fingers as she continued to cover her face. She couldn't just lie here. She had to do something.

She looked around and noticed that the majority of the crows were now on the ground or their victims. They had almost entirely neglected the area where she, her mother and Lisowski had been cowering. She supposed they were attacking the more exposed targets first – they were scavengers, after all. She moved her leg, kicking Lisowski below his knee. He looked around to her.

"Do you have anything? A weapon?" she said, her breath faster and shallower than she'd first realised.

The farmer shook his head. "I didn't bring my rifle to the village, if that's what you mean." He gave her a knowing smile, in spite of the horror of the situation. "But what about noise? Birds like this hate noise." He glanced over to the postmaster's wife, Natalia following his gaze. They watched as she rolled from her back on to her front, her arms flailing as the birds soared before crashing down onto her, pecking and clawing at her head, staining her coiled silver hair a bright crimson.

Natalia looked back to Lisowski. "We have to try." She pushed her hands to the ground and heaved herself up, Liswoski and her mother doing the same. They ran over to the scene of the attack, clapping their hands and shouting. Natalia aimed a kick at one of the crows as it ripped another strand of flesh from the neck of Father Mateusz and it fell back, wings flapping, its own neck grotesquely twisted. It tried to fly away but couldn't lift itself. It hopped towards the edge of the square. She reached down, helping up the priest, and pointed to the post office. He held his hands over his bloody face and nodded, running across the square, the doctor hobbling behind, his glasses broken and arms wheeling at yet more of the smaller crows and jackdaws that continued to attack him.

Natalia looked around to see her mother, who, having gathered up stones, was tossing them at the raven which was still pinning the butcher. One made contact, the bird bringing up its huge wings to protect itself as more of the tiny rocks pelted it.

Lisowski cried out in delight as he made contact with the depleted flock of birds that still flew in seemingly random patterns. Natalia watched as he used a piece of wood he had prised up from a sign outside the general store, sweeping it through the fast-moving black mass, handfuls of birds shrieking out in a shrill voice as they rolled to the ground, their wings rendered useless by the force of the impact.

"We're winning! I think we might be able to save everyone!" the farmer said as he struck another group and watched them scatter to the ground, fidgeting as they tried in vain to launch themselves back into the air.

"Think again!" Natalia's mother groaned and pointed to the edge of the town square. Natalia froze as she saw two fully grown wolves stalking towards them, their bodies low to the ground, ears pinned back, ready to attack.

"Even worse," said Natalia, gesturing towards the space between the pub — still overgrown with plants — and the butcher's shop. From the gap stepped the big cat she recognised from Baba Yaga's house and another, seemingly younger lynx. Each was prepared to attack, their eyes almost black, mouths open, displaying their razor-sharp teeth.

The four animals stalked forward, the handful of people who remained in the square looking one way and the other.

"What do we do now?" Natalia cried out. She looked to her mother and then to Lisowski. Each of them remained silent, watching as the predators edged closer.

Lisowski was the first to act, he stepped forward and swung with the length of wood he'd been using to attack the birds, aiming for the leading wolf. The animal leapt forward, clearing three metres and more in a lightning-fast single bound. It fixed the wood in its jaws and twisted its head, wrenching it from Lisowski's hands and throwing him off balance.

The second wolf wasted no time in lurching forward, jaws wide open. Natalia watched, mouth agape and unable to move, the saliva from the wolf's mouth seemingly drifting through the air in slow motion. The animal's jaws closed, clamped around the farmer's arm. She moved closer, finding her strength after first being so utterly paralysed by the sight of the wolves' attack. She screamed, but the wolves paid her no heed, the first one chomping through the wooden weapon and the second already tearing the fabric of Lisowski's jacket. The first signs of blood exploded in a fine mist that coloured the grey cobblestones of the square. The farmer wound up and punched the wolf on the snout, causing it to release its grip for a moment, but it quickly bit down again, the sound of teeth grinding through meat and onto bone audible from where Natalia stood.

Her own scream was drowned out by that of her mother, causing her to spin around. The postmaster's wife lay on her back, the younger of the two lynxes standing over her, its clawed paws swiping at her abdomen and working its way through the fabric of her clothes. The older lynx – the one which had been so close to Natalia just days earlier – stood watch beside the scene on its haunches, ready to attack.

Natalia began to feel sick and dizzy, looking this

way and that at the scene of destruction. Nature truly was going to wipe out the village in its entirety; there was nothing any of them could do. She felt her head spin, her heart thumping, and then she saw what would push her over the edge. The raven stood with its long black toes holding down the butcher's face, then jerked its body down, its beak digging down into his mouth. It pulled up and a sliver of the man's tongue was ripped free, blood spurting from the wound and onto his face and chest as his heart thumped.

Now she was broken. She looked back to Lisowski, still battling to keep the wolves away as they shredded the skin and flesh of his arm. She spun to the postmaster's wife and saw the paw of the lynx break through her underclothes and tear into the flesh of her abdomen, three lines of bright blood painting stripes on the ground beside her from the lynx's claws. Natalia bent over and vomited, everything she'd eaten that day forcing its way back up her throat, the taste of burning acid with it. As she stood up, she felt her head get lighter. Her vision blurred and she fell onto her side, chin smashing on the hard ground, cracking open. She lay on her side, her eyes flicking from Lisowski's battle with the wolves, to the postmaster's wife being sliced open, and finally to the trickle of her own blood running between the cracks in the cobblestones. She whispered a prayer.

Then the animals stopped. The birds settled on

the ground before the flock dispersed, the gathered corvids flying off in all directions, out of sight. The wolves and lynxes drew back from their victims, still maintaining eye contact. Natalia lifted her head from the cold stone and glanced around. Everything was still. The victims of the animals' attacks twitched and writhed in pain, their clothing tattered and soaked with blood. Everything else was still. The wind had died down, the pealing of the bells had been silenced.

Suddenly the larger lynx moved, calmly walking away from the church and towards the edge of the village. Natalia watched it walk further and further away until it reached a solitary, cloaked figure, standing at the entrance to the square. The person was short, holding a long branch of wood, which looked like a staff of some kind. To the top, they had attached a polished bird skull, though she was too far away to make out what kind of bird it might belong to. The lynx approached them and the figure outstretched a hand. The big cat leaned in and nuzzled it, the fingers of the hand rubbing at the tufts at the side of its face.

The figure lowered its hand, then spoke. "I, Baba Yaga, the balance between humankind and the wild, call for this conflict to stop."

Silence. Nothing moved.

"In order for the debt to the spirit of the wilderness to be paid, just one single life need be taken."

Natalia looked up at the figure, the hood of the heavy brown cloak still obscuring its features. She dragged herself to her feet and went to her mother, wrapping her arms around her. She looked back over her shoulder at the hooded figure – the Baba Yaga – and yelled, "You can't take her! It wasn't her fault!"

Baba Yaga released its grip on the staff, the wood making a loud, clattering sound that echoed across the square in the oppressive silence. It reached up and tugged at its hood. It pulled it back and down, then shook his shaggy, sandy-coloured hair.

"It's the only way, sister," said Kuba. "The wilderness spirit came to me in a dream and told me that if I took the place of the Baba Yaga, I could save everyone. Everyone except mother. It's the *only* way."

Natalia dropped to her knees. "Brother, it's not possible. You'll kill your own mother? *Our* mother? You can't. You simply can't."

Kuba shook his head. "Natka, first of all, *I* won't kill her. One of these fabulous beasts will." He reached out and fussed the lynx once again. "And secondly, did Baba Yaga deserve to die? What had she done that was so terrible? Save my leg? Save my *life*? And all because *our* mother was afraid of the devil. I've spoken to the wilderness spirit and it is *far* older than the devil, *and* your God, for that matter." He cast a dismissive glance up at the church tower, looming over the square, then looked back to his sister.

Their mother stepped forward, standing in front of Natalia now. She spoke to Kuba. "My son, I did what I thought was right. I'm a Catholic woman and I was always suspicious of that witch. I couldn't bear the thought of you being led in to Satanism or... I don't know. I ask you to forgive me, but, if you cannot, I would rather I die than the whole village be wiped out." She stepped back to stand beside her daughter, putting her arm around her shoulder and kissing her on the top of her head.

Kuba smiled, a broad grin that amplified his youth, then crouched down to retrieve his staff. He held up the skull – clearly that of a jackdaw, Natalia saw, now that she was closer to him – and looked into the hollows of the skull's eyes. He whispered something under his breath, then lowered it again. There was a long silence, accompanied by the sound of the new spring leaves in the trees rustling in the breeze. Kuba took a step forward, holding his staff out in front of him.

"I understand your reasons, Mother, and I understand your mind was poisoned against the balance by the teachings of your faith. You ask me to forgive you, and forgive you I do." He bowed his head, closing his eyes.

Their mother brought her hands up to cover her mouth and began to weep. She tried to find the words to thank him, but they came out unintelligibly through her sobs. She opened her arms and stepped forward. As she did so, the lead wolf sprang through the air, opening its jaws wide apart before it clamped them down on her throat. Her body tilted backwards, and she seemed to hang, suspended in the air for a long, drawn out moment.

Natalia opened her mouth to scream, but no words came. She watched, paralysed, as a thin cloud of blood hissed from her mother's torn throat, before the older woman's body crumpled to the ground. She lay there, her arms still open in readiness for an embrace from her son, while her body convulsed as her life seeped away through the ravages of her neck.

"I forgive you, but the wilderness spirit cannot," Kuba said, turning and beginning to walk away, towards the forest.

Natalia shrieked and ran towards him, her arms high above her head, ready to strike, but Lisowski dashed to her and grabbed her in his bloodied arms, restraining her, not letting her move. "The beasts will take you as well, girl. Let him go. Let him *go*."

Natalia's body went limp, like a rag doll in the farmer's arms. She sobbed violently as he held her. When she opened her eyes, she saw the blood that had pooled around her mother. She lay still, her eyes wide open but glassy, devoid of life.

ABOUT THE AUTHOR

Kev Harrison is a writer and English language teacher from the UK, living in Lisbon Portugal. He previously lived in Poland for three years where the gestation for scenes and characters for this book began. He primarily writes horror but also dabbles in sci-fi, urban fantasy and more, all with a decidedly dark tone. His short fiction has been featured in the anthologies *Lost Films* from Perpetual Motion Machine Publishing, *In Darkness, Delight,* from Corpus Press, *We Shall Be Monsters* from Renaissance Press and many more. You can find him on twitter as @lisboetaingles and at www.kevharrisonfiction.com